# CAVANAUGH'S
# SECRET DELIVERY

MARIE FERRARELLA

**MILLS & BOON**

First Published in Great Britain 2018
by Mills & Boon, an imprint of HarperCollins*Publishers*
1 London Bridge Street, London, SE1 9GF

*Cavanaugh's Secret Delivery* © 2018 Marie Rydzynski-Ferrarella

ISBN: 978-0-263-26585-9

39-0718

MIX
Paper from
responsible sources
FSC® C007454

FSC
www.fsc.org

To
Tiffany Khauo-Melgar
With Love

# *Chapter One*

Man, he'd really needed this night out, Detective Dugan Cavanaugh thought. He loved his job, no question about it, but after putting in what felt like three weeks straight to get all those slippery little ducks in a row, it really felt good to unwind and blow off some steam tonight, even for a little while.

However, the problem with blowing off steam was that sometimes time did manage to get away from him. Like tonight. It was ten after midnight.

He really hadn't intended to be out this late.

"And tomorrow is a school day," he chuckled to himself under his breath. That meant that he couldn't sleep in—not that he even knew how at this point in his life. "Time to get you home, Detective Cavanaugh, before you suddenly turn into that pumpkin that your mama used to read to you about way back when."

Dugan grinned to himself. Anyone overhearing him would have thought he was three sheets to the wind. Truth was, he wasn't even quite one sheet. Despite coming out to Malone's and hoisting a few beers, he wasn't drunk, just feeling very good.

And relaxed.

But he wasn't intoxicated. Dugan knew better than to get behind the wheel of his car if he were. The beers, both of them, had been consumed over the course of six hours, and given the fact that he was six-three and had a physique that would have made a bodybuilder envious, those beers had less than no effect on him. It just felt good to get together with a number of his friends and family.

This was what it was all about for him, Dugan thought. Friends and family. And keeping the world safe for those friends and family—as well as the public at large.

But right now, it was time to go home and get some very well-deserved sleep so that tomorrow morning, he could get up and do it all again. For him, as well as most of the members of his family, that meant finding ways to put the bad guys away—the faster the better. In his particular case, that involved getting the goods on drug dealers.

He stifled a yawn. Man, he was more tired than he thought, Dugan realized. He'd also parked his car farther away than he'd thought. But when he'd arrived six hours ago, the parking lot behind the bar was packed and there were cars lining both sides of the street. It turned out that there was an impromptu bachelor party being held at the bar, so the place was really packed. That made the owner quite happy, Dugan thought, remembering the wide grin on the former police officer's face as the man tended bar. But the extra customers had made parking a particular challenge.

"Maybe I'll walk off some of those calories from the beer," Dugan murmured as he crossed what was normally a busy intersection. At the moment, the streets were totally deserted.

His upbeat attitude was due to the fact that he'd been taught to always look at the bright side of things, even when things appeared to be dark and bleak. It was something his late mother, Eva, had instilled in him, as well as in his three younger brothers, and while none of them could be accused of being mindlessly happy-go-lucky, her philosophy had helped all of them weather the personal storms that came their way.

There it was, Dugan thought, finally sighting his pride and joy, an old 1965 Mustang he had personally rebuilt and restored over the course of three summer vacations in between juggling part time jobs while he was going to college.

A warm feeling filled him the way it always did whenever he looked at the cherry-red product of all his hard work.

"I'm almost there, old girl," he said, as if the car could hear him. "Almost—"

A screeching sound suddenly disrupted the otherwise still April night.

Dugan stopped short, instantly alert—just in case. Turning his head toward the sound, he listened, trying to discern where it was coming from and, more importantly, what it was.

Was that awful noise coming from a cat being attacked or—

The sound came again, louder this time and definitely filled with agony. It wasn't a cat, it was human—of a sort.

It was the kind of sound that, had he been lost in the Alaskan wilderness, he would have attributed to coming from a Yeti, a mythical creature sometimes equated with the equally mythical Big Foot.

All this was going through Dugan's head at lightning speed as Dugan broke into a run, heading toward the source of the unearthly screeching.

In short order, he realized that the gut-wrenching noise was coming from a car that was pulled up, askew, against a curb in an alley that was a block away from where his own car was.

The car's lights were on, but the engine appeared to be off.

Another scream, even more powerful this time, ripped though the air. Dugan pulled out his weapon just before he reached the vehicle.

Cautiously, not knowing what he was about to find, he looked into the car and saw a woman, gripping the steering wheel. Her face was contorted with pain and she was screaming. There was a gun lying on the passenger seat beside her.

She also had to be the most pregnant woman he had ever seen.

Dugan knew he was taking a chance.

Ordinarily, a gun on the scene demanded that certain protocol be adhered to. But unless the woman was smuggling a double order of watermelons, she appeared to be in just too much pain to be a threat. She certainly didn't look like any drug dealer he had ever come across.

So, taking a breath, he lowered his weapon and rapped on her partially opened window to get her attention.

"Ma'am? Do you need help?"

The woman instantly jerked at the sound of his deep male voice, looking his way. Fear telegraphed through her with the speed of a lightning bolt.

She was not about to die in this car tonight, she thought.

Working her way through the searing pain, she reached toward the gun on the passenger seat, stretching and groaning.

Dugan reached in through the open window even though it was tricky and managed to grab the gun before the woman could get her fingers around it.

"Give…me…that!" she managed to grind out. She was breathing hard now and every word took effort. She felt as though her dark blond hair was plastered against her forehead. Even the top of her head felt as if it was coming off at any second.

"Look, lady, I heard you shrieking and I came to see if I could help, but I'd like not to get my head blown off while I'm doing it." Dugan saw the terror in her face. It was after midnight and she was alone. He couldn't really blame her. "I'm a cop," he added, hoping that would reassure her.

She definitely didn't believe him. "No…you're… NOT!"

The woman had one hell of a set of lungs on her, Dugan thought, opening the passenger door. Rather than argue with her, in the interest of expediency, he took out his badge and showed it to her.

"See?" he asked her.

She still wasn't convinced. "You…could have… gotten…that…in any…toy store," she bit off.

"Fair enough." He took out his ID next and held it up almost in front of her face. The woman was sweating profusely, he noted. This had to hurt like hell, he thought. "Okay?" he asked, nodding at his wallet.

"O…kay," she panted. Her eyes widened as she saw him get in and reach over to her seat belt, releasing it. She was wary again and there was nowhere to retreat. "What…are…you…doing?" she demanded with as much indignation as she could manage.

Before he could answer, she shrieked again, pushing against the floor with her feet as she arched back in the seat now that she was no longer restricted by the seat belt.

It didn't help. Nothing helped. The pain just couldn't be escaped.

"I can't help you from outside the car," Dugan told the woman.

"Get…away!" she ordered, panting so hard she was getting dizzy. It took everything she had to keep from passing out.

"Don't worry," he told her, "neither one of us wants to be here, but you need help and I'm the only one around." He weighed his options, then shook his head. "I don't think I can get you to the hospital in time. If it'll make you feel any better, my aunt drives an ambulance."

He was talking about Aunt Maeve and she actually owned the company at this point, but he didn't think the pregnant woman was in any condition to listen to any lengthy explanations. Not the way she was screaming and certainly not the way she was arching her back and moving from side to side. The simplest explanation was the best one.

"She taught all of us a few basic emergency procedures," he told the pregnant woman in a calm, friendly voice. "One of which was what to do when a woman went into intense labor."

There was still skepticism in her eyes. "You… swear?" she demanded.

He told himself that she was scared and that made him feel for her. "I swear," he told her with all the solemnity he could manage.

"O-KAY!" she screamed.

Her contractions were coming closer and closer.

There was hardly any time between them at this point. And this time, because he was close, she grabbed his hand and held on to it so hard Dugan thought his fingers were going to snap off.

When the contraction passed and she breathed a little more regularly, she released his hand.

Dugan flexed his fingers, surprised that he still could. "Hell of a grip you have there. What is your name, anyway?" he asked.

He could tell by the way she was breathing that she was bracing herself. The next second, she was being seized by yet another massive contraction.

"Scarlet," she managed to say just before she was once again writhing in pain.

She'd grabbed his hand again. This time he tried to go with it, waiting it out and hoping he still had use of his fingers when she finally let go. He felt really awful for her, and not too keen for himself, either.

Dugan looked toward the backseat. It looked relatively empty. If he could just get this woman to go into the back, it would be better for both of them, given the situation.

"Ideally, we should get you into the backseat. There's a little more room to work with—"

By the time the words were out of his mouth, she was arching her back again and definitely trying to get away from the pain, even as she tried not to scream at the top of her lungs.

"I'll take that as a no." Dugan rethought the situation. He had to work with what he had. "Okay, I need you to lie on your back."

She was huffing, trying not to push. She didn't want her baby born in a rental car. That wasn't right. It was bad enough that it had been conceived in one. Her eyes shifted toward the cop.

"That's…how… I…got…this…WAY!" she ground out.

He could tell that she wasn't very happy with him. "You know, if this was just eight hours from now, that scream of yours would have brought a whole bunch of people running, but right now, I'm all you've got, so let's see if we can get this done as painlessly as possible."

Too late Dugan realized what he'd said. "Sorry, wrong choice of words. Just lie back," he told her again. "Please."

This time, she listened.

He left the passenger door open so that he had some space to do what he needed to do. She didn't even seem to notice.

"Okay, I apologize ahead of time," he told her.

She was moaning loudly, trying her best not to scream, and he doubted if she'd really heard him, but that didn't matter. He'd said it just to make sure he was covered.

As swiftly as possible, he got rid of her underwear, pushed back the oversized blouse that was covering her swollen belly and took a closer look at what he was up against.

"Good news, you're crowning," he told her.

Her eyes felt wet and there was a ringing noise in her ears. She tried to concentrate on what he was telling her.

"What's…that?"

He looked up and tried to smile encouragingly at her. "It means that you're going to be a mama soon," Dugan said.

That wasn't good enough. This pain was ripping her in half. "HOW… SOOON?"

"Very soon," he assured her. "As a matter of fact, it won't be long now," he said, feeling almost as amazed as he figured she probably was right about now. *Hope you were right, Aunt Maeve.* "Okay, Scarlet, when I tell you to push, I want you to push. Push!" he ordered.

The woman grabbed on to part of the steering wheel with one hand and the back of the headrest with the other. Breathing hard, she arched and pushed down hard for all she was worth.

Mentally, Dugan counted up to five.

"Okay, stop. Stop!" he ordered her again when she didn't. "Scarlet, I know this is hard, but you have to stop when I tell you to stop," Dugan told the frazzled woman.

The look she gave him said a lot more than she was able to at this point. It didn't take him much to fill in the blanks.

"Yes, I know, it's your body, you're in pain and I'm just the jerk issuing orders. But if you push too hard, you're going to wind up tearing things I can't repair here," he warned her. "Do you understand what I'm saying to you?"

Her eyes were on him and then she finally nodded.

"Okay, ready?" he asked. She looked at him with wide eyes and he told her, "Push!"

"I...*am*!" she cried, squeezing her eyes closed as she pushed down for all she was worth.

She fully expected this to be it—but it wasn't.

She fell back against the seat cushion, breathing hard and ready to give up.

As if sensing what was going on through her head, Dugan told her, "You can do this, Scarlet. You know you can. C'mon, just one more time."

"I...don't...believe...you," she whimpered, panting and trying very hard to catch her breath.

Her head was spinning, making her feel as if she was going to go on like this forever, in pain and pushing until she died.

"C'mon, Scarlet, you're made of better stuff than this. Just one more time," Dugan urged her, repeating the words he'd already used.

"I...hate...you!"

"I can live with that," he told her. "Now push!" he ordered.

She had no choice. It was as if the baby had taken control of her instead of the other way around. The baby was pushing its way out.

"It's...*coming*!"

"It sure is," Dugan agreed, excited. "One more push," he told her. "Just one more—that's it," he encouraged. "That's it!"

And then, just like that, he found himself holding a baby in his hands. For a second, Dugan was in complete, mind-numbing awe.

Despite everything he'd told her, he had never been in this position before. He'd never actually had to put his training—which was far from recent—to use like this before.

And then Dugan came to life.

"Here," he told the brand-new mother, placing the baby on her stomach. "Hold her and don't move," he ordered.

"It's a girl?" the woman asked him, relief highlighted in her face.

"Oh, yeah," he answered, realizing that he hadn't said that before. "It's a girl."

The next moment, he was taking out a knife from his pocket. It had been a gift from his mother for his fourteenth birthday, the last gift she had ever given him and he was never without it.

"Do you have a paperclip?" he asked the new mother.

She was holding the baby in her arms, totally stunned and totally in love with the baby girl she was holding. She blinked as she looked up at him.

"A what?"

"A paperclip," he repeated. "I'm going to need something to temporarily stem any blood that might start flowing from the cut." Dugan was already several steps ahead in his mind.

"What blood?" she asked, looking at the baby, panicking. "Is there blood?"

"No, but there will be when I cut the cord," he told her.

"Oh." She thought for a moment, then asked, "Will a hairclip do?"

He put his hand out. "It might. Let me see it."

"It's in my hair," the woman told him. She was still having trouble catching her breath. "You're going to have to get it out," she told him, almost apologizing. "My hands are full."

He grinned at her. "Right."

Leaning over the baby and looking closely at the new mother's head, he saw the hairclip. She'd had it loosely holding back her dark-blond hair. He took it out as best he could, trying not to pull. He failed.

"Sorry," he apologized for the umpteenth time. "Got it," he told her. "Okay, now for the last part."

She eyed the knife, her apprehension growing again. "Is this going to hurt her?"

"No, I don't think so."

Dugan said it in such a way that she felt she could believe him. "Okay," she said tentatively.

Taking the knife back in his hand, he quickly cut the cord, then swiftly placed the hairclip just at the baby's end of it. Once he was sure the clip would hold—he watched it for a minute—he stripped off his hoodie.

"Now what are you doing?" the woman asked him, not sure what to think.

He had delivered her baby, but she knew nothing about this man, other than he'd said he was a cop. Maybe he was and maybe he wasn't. But even if he was one, that still wasn't enough to convince her that everything else was all right.

She looked up at him now, wondering if she could get away with her baby if she had to.

"It's chilly," Dugan told her. "The baby's going to need something wrapped around her while we wait for the ambulance," he explained.

"The ambulance?" she repeated. She'd forgotten about that. Forgotten about everything except for this baby she was now holding.

"Unless you'd rather stay here for a while," Dugan told her, looking perfectly serious.

No, it was definitely better for her to be around other people. "No, I—"

"I'm kidding, Scarlet," he told her, waving away his previous words. "Just hang on. We'll get you and your girl to the hospital and all of this will seem like just one bad dream," he promised.

"No, I didn't mean that—" the woman began, but Dugan was already on the phone.

Holding up his hand as a silent request that she should hang on to her thoughts until he was able to get off the phone, he started to talk to the person on the other end.

"Nine-one-one, what's your emergency?" a female dispatcher asked.

"This is Detective Dugan Cavanaugh," he said, then gave the woman on the other end of the phone his badge number. "I need a bus sent out right away to the corner of Dyer and Santa Rosa. I've got a mother and a baby here." He smiled at them as he said it. "The city just gained a new citizen about three minutes ago. Mother and baby seem to be doing fine, but I'll leave that up to you to determine," he told dispatch.

"Very good, detective. I can have an ambulance out there within the next ten minutes. Will you be there, as well?" she asked.

"Got nowhere else to be," he answered, still looking at the woman and the baby he had helped to bring into the world.

"Fine. Ten minutes," the woman repeated, then ended the call.

"Are you coming with me?" the new mother asked, looking at him above her mewling baby.

"Unless you'd rather end our beautiful friendship right here," he said, giving her the option.

"No," she answered. And then, in words that had been entirely unfamiliar to her these last few years, she said, "I'd like you to come."

"Then I will," he told her. Cocking his head, he listened for a second, then said, "I think the ambulance's already coming. Must be a slow night," he told her with a wink.

Just then, as the baby began to cry, he felt his phone ringing. "I think I spoke too soon," he said as he took out his cell phone and looked at the call number on the screen. "Yup, I spoke too soon."

The number on the screen was one he knew very well.

# Chapter Two

"Dugan Cavanaugh," Dugan said as he answered the phone.

"We've got a problem, Cavanaugh," the voice on the other end of the line told him. It was the detective he'd been partnered for over the last year and a half, Jason Nguyen.

Dugan watched as he saw the ambulance pulling up into the alley. "Now?"

"No, tomorrow," Jason answered. "Of course now. Look, tell the honey you're with you'll get back to her as soon as you can, but that something's come up and you need to go."

"For your information," Dugan informed the other detective, "I'm not with a 'honey.'"

"Good, then that'll make it easier for you to get

over here," Jason said. Dugan could hear noise in the background, but he refrained from asking what was going on. Jason had a habit of leaving no detail untold if he could possible help it.

"Look," Jason was saying, "I don't like getting up out of a dead sleep, either, but you need to have gotten your tail out here at least five minutes ago."

The ambulance had arrived and the paramedics were getting out. Dugan silently waved the two men over toward the woman's car even though he was still on the phone.

"Why?" he asked, asking Jason. "What won't keep until tomorrow morning?"

"Mitch Gomez was just fished out of the lake twenty minutes ago," Jason answered flatly.

"That'll do it." Dugan didn't have to ask if the man was dead. Nguyen wouldn't be calling him if he wasn't. "Where are you?" He paused as the other detective rattled off the address. "I'll be there as soon as I can," Dugan said grimly.

He terminated the call and put the phone back in his pocket.

Meanwhile, the two paramedics were bringing around the gurney. "You the father?" the paramedic closest to him, Jeff, asked.

Still in the vehicle, the woman cried, "No, he's not!"

Dugan shook his head. "Just a Good Samaritan in the right place at the right time," he told the paramedic.

"Don't worry, ma'am, we'll get you and your baby to the hospital quickly," the other paramedic, Nathan according to his tag, was saying to the woman. Before he tried to get her and her baby out of the car, he looked back toward Dugan. "Are you coming with her, Good Samaritan?" he asked.

The next moment, he handed the baby over to his partner and then he took the woman gently into his arms. With a minimum of effort, he transferred her carefully to the gurney.

"Something I have to do first," Dugan answered the paramedic. When both the new mother, now on the gurney, and the paramedic looked at him, Dugan explained, "I'm a cop. Something's come up." Turning his attention toward the woman he'd just aided, he told her, "But I'll be there as soon as I can."

"Okay," she said, nodding.

Dugan had a feeling she didn't believe him, but there was nothing he could do about that right now. All that mattered was that she was in safe hands and that was all that really counted, anyway.

"I'll see you later," he told the new mother as he watched the paramedics place her gurney in the back of the ambulance.

"Right, later," she replied, then added, "Don't worry about it."

Dugan frowned. He should have called his aunt's ambulance, he thought as he watched the paramedics close the doors and then round to the front of the vehicle. He knew all the drivers there. But there was nothing he could do about that now.

Dugan sprang into action. He quickly closed up

the woman's car and then, finally, ran to his own a block away.

Starting it up, he took out the detachable light and stuck it on top of the roof. He didn't like doing it to the Mustang, but the situation was dire and he needed to get there ASAP.

He still couldn't believe that Gomez was dead. He'd only managed to finally talk the guy into being his confidential informant less than a month ago.

"I don't think he ever knew what hit him," Jason said as he stood there, looking down at the sprawled-out body lying before him.

Dugan had managed to get there in record time. Luckily, at this time of night, most of Aurora's citizens were asleep and traffic was close to non-existent except for a few hotspots. As it was, this had happened near the lake that was located in the next town. By the time he had gotten there, Mitch Gomez's body had not only been fished out, it was now about to be taken away by the medical examiner.

Dugan had arrived just in time to see the ME begin to zip up the black body bag. Stopping the man, he looked down at Gomez's lifeless face.

"Three shots to the back of the head," Jason told him. "Execution style."

Dugan blew out a breath. "Damn. Any chance we can get jurisdiction over the body?" he asked.

The medical examiner didn't answer him. Instead, he just finished closing up the bag, then with the help of his assistant, he took it away.

Jason was left to answer the question. "Hey, it happened here, away from Aurora, but I don't think they're going to fight you for it if you want to claim the body as ours. Just remember, it becomes *our* unsolved murder," the detective told Dugan. "Not exactly brownie points for that as far as I can see if we *don't* solve it." He looked at Dugan closely. "You sure you want to do this?"

"He was my CI," Dugan said, looking at the body as it was being taken away. "Hell, he wasn't even old enough to legally drink," he added, shaking his head. The next moment, he went after the ME and said, "Leave it here. We'll take the body."

The medical examiner shrugged his shoulders. "Suit yourself. I've got more than enough bodies in the morgue as it is," he told Dugan. "Leave it," he said to his assistant.

"He wasn't legally old enough to do any of the things he did, but that didn't keep him from doing it," Jason told his partner. "Hey, it's not your fault," he said, seeing the look on Dugan's face.

"I know that. But it still seems like a huge waste. I can't help but feel being my CI was what got him killed," Dugan murmured. He took out his phone in order to call their medical examiner and tell her that they had another body.

"Yeah, well, he knew what he was doing," Jason argued.

"Doc? Sorry to get you up at such an ungodly hour, but we've got a body for you."

"Flowers would have been nicer," the voice on

the other end of the line mumbled. He heard another voice in the distance asking something. "I think it's one of your cousins," Kristin, the head medical examiner said, answering the other voice. "He's trying to cull my favor with a body." Returning to phone, she said, "Okay, give me the address. I'll be there as soon as I can."

Dugan gave the woman the address then terminated the call. Tucking the phone away, he looked back at the body, hidden now beneath the black body bag.

He had caught the one-time college student on a possessions charge and managed to flip him when Gomez said he had current intel he could trade. It turned out to be good information. Better than Dugan had thought, at first. So good, apparently, that it had wound up costing his confidential informant his life.

"I don't think he did know what he was doing," Dugan said thoughtfully, referring to what Jason had said before he called Kristin. "I think that he thought it was all going to go his way and turn out the way he wanted in the end."

Looking at the black body bag, Jason shrugged. "Nothing we can do about it now."

"Except catch the son of a bitch who killed him," Dugan pointed out, saying the words with such a passion it caused Jason to look at him uncertainly.

"Yeah, there's that, too," Jason agreed, trying to lighten the mood. "Hey, I really didn't roust you out of the arms of some nubile young woman?" Jason asked, curious.

"Actually, I had just finished delivering a baby when you called me," Dugan answered, turning away from the body.

Rather than say anything, Jason just started to laugh. "Yeah, right."

"No, I'm serious. When you called, I had just finished delivering this woman's baby and there was an ambulance on its way to take her to Aurora Memorial," Dugan said, mentioning the name of the closest hospital to that particular place, which was also known as the best one in the county.

Jason began to laugh again, but this time, his laughter was very short-lived. He paused, looking at his partner. Dugan wasn't even smiling. Dugan usually smiled by now if he was putting him on.

Jason eyed his partner. "You're serious."

"You already asked me that," Dugan pointed out. In the back of his head, he couldn't help thinking that one life had just ended while another life had just started. He supposed that was what real life was all about, but somehow, it still didn't really feel like things equaled out.

"Yeah, but I didn't think—damn, a baby," Jason repeated, shaking his head and grinning. "So? How did it feel?" he asked.

"Well, it all happened so fast, I didn't have time to think or feel anything," Dugan admitted. "And by the time I could, I was already on my way to the scene of the crime."

"And she's no relation? Not a girlfriend or a...?" Jason let his voice drift off as he looked at Dugan, waiting for the other detective to fill in the blank about the woman's relationship to him.

"No, not a girlfriend or a…" Dugan repeated. "I was going toward my car when I heard this unearthly scream. I looked to see where it was coming from. This woman was sitting in her car, looking like she was about to pop at any second."

"So you delivered the baby?" Jason asked, as if he was trying to wrap his head around the whole scenario.

"Well, I started out to do that," Dugan answered. "But she actually wound up delivering the baby on her own for the most part."

"Wow." Jason shook his head, envious of the experience. "All I did after I left the bar tonight was finish up the puzzle I was working on for the last week and a half," he admitted quietly. "You going to go there now? To the hospital?" Jason prompted when Dugan just looked at him blankly.

"No, not until we file all the paperwork on this," Dugan answered. "He was my CI."

"Nobody else knows that yet," Jason pointed out. "You don't have to do that part right now."

"*I* know that," Dugan said pointedly. "But I will. It's only right."

Jason sighed, shaking his head. "Are all you Cavanaughs such sticklers for honesty when it comes to crossing your T's and dotting your I's?" the other detective asked. "Don't any of you ever kick back?"

"Not where it counts," Dugan answered, then added with a grin, "Lucky for you."

Jason laughed. He saw the point. "Yeah, I guess you're right."

"Okay," Dugan said, taking a breath and telling himself that they were going to need a fresh start here. "Let's see what we can find out about this murder. Before homicide starts horning in on our case."

Jason looked almost hangdog. "So much for going home tonight."

Dugan paused to look at the other detective. "Hey, you called me, remember?"

Jason looked resigned—for now. "I guess I've got nobody else to blame but myself for being here," he replied. Then his eyes glimmered a little. "But even so, I can still try to put the blame on you for my sleepless night."

Dugan laughed. "Okay. Whatever floats your boat, Nguyen."

Dugan didn't get to the hospital that morning. Nor did he managed to get there the whole day. The investigation into Gomez's murder kept him and Nguyen busy.

It wasn't until the following morning that he finally managed to scrape together a little time for himself. He used it to swing by the hospital.

On his way over to Aurora Memorial Hospital, he decided to give himself a total of fifteen minutes there. Twenty at the most.

Despite the fact that it was only eight in the morning, finding somewhere to park was a bit of a challenge—at least, if he wanted to park somewhere close to the front. The hospital always seemed to be busy.

He wound up parking toward the very back of the lot. Because he was short on time, he decided to sprint. He told himself that a quick sprint would be good for him. It was either that or drive around a few times until someone decided to free up a spot and leave. He didn't have time for that.

The city had too many people, he thought, getting out of his car. Used to be, according to his uncles—at least, the ones who had been born in this city—that Aurora was so small it hardly warranted a hospital at all, much less two.

It had been a huge deal when the second hospital, Aurora Memorial was finally opened. At the time, the hospital was half the size it was now and there had been empty beds on occasion. But that was because the city hadn't done all the growing that it had of late. Back then, it was more like a one-horse town than a city.

He smiled to himself. According to his uncles, there'd been three lights down the main drag. One at one freeway, one at the other and one that was halfway in between.

There'd been cows here instead of all these people, and crime had been almost nothing. Now the cows were gone and crime was on its way up, although he and the rest of the Aurora Police Force were definitely trying to do something about that.

*Okay, this is supposed to be your downtime, Dugan, remember? No shop talk, just a nice, quick*

*visit. Something to remind you that you're capable
of doing good deeds once in a while and you're not
just a police detective, but a human being as well.*

Approaching the main doors, Dugan waited until
they sprang open. He preferred opening his own
doors, but progress seemed to have other ideas, so
he waited. Once the doors had pulled apart, slowly,
he walked into the hospital.

The last time he had been here, everything had
looked different. But the hospital had gone through
a new wave of building again, or modernizing, as it
were. For one thing, the lobby didn't look the way
it used to.

It took him a moment to get his bearings. Looking around, he finally spotted the information desk.
Relieved, he approached the two people who were
sitting there—a man and a woman—looking more
than a little bored. They both came alive when they
saw him.

"May we help you?" the attendants asked almost
in unison.

"I need to get to the maternity floor," Dugan told
them.

"That would be the third floor," the young woman
said, smiling at him.

As he began to walk away, the male attendant
called after him. "If you give us the patient's name,
we can tell you which room she is in. It'll make it
go faster for you."

"Okay."

Backing up, Dugan returned to the desk and then

looked for a way to say this that didn't make him look like some kind of mindless fool.

"Well, this is a little awkward because I just know her first name." He saw the two attendants exchange looks and he could almost guess what they were thinking. "No, it's not like that," he assured them. "I'm a cop. She went into labor in her car. I happen to be passing by so I helped her give birth."

"All right," the male attendant, Dale, said guardedly. "What's the woman's *first* name?"

"Her name's Scarlet," Dugan told him.

Dale skimmed down the screen, then looked up, a slightly dubious expression on his gaunt face. "I'm sorry but there's no one named Scarlet registered at the hospital."

"Look again," Dugan instructed, feeling exasperated. "She was admitted with her baby a little after midnight two days ago. The ambulance brought her here."

Looking really skeptical at this point, Dale skimmed over the names a second time. "Sorry," he announced. "No Scarlet."

"Let me look," the second attendant, Rita, said, taking over the screen. Her superior attitude vanished quickly. Looking up, she shook her head. "I'm sorry but he's right. There is no one named Scarlet on the maternity floor."

Dugan frowned at the two attendants at the reception desk. "That doesn't make any sense. Maybe she had complications and she was admitted to another division," he suggested. "Look to see if there was anyone admitted to any other section of the hospital by the name of Scarlet."

"That is highly irregular," Dale informed him, taking umbrage. However, the look that Dugan shot at him had the attendant quickly skimming through the records. Finishing, he shook his head. "No, I'm sorry. There was no Scarlet admitted to the hospital in the last two days on any of the floors."

"All right, maybe they made a mistake with her name," Dugan said. "Was there *anyone* admitted a little after midnight two days ago to the maternity floor? She had a newborn daughter." He knew that at least that much was right.

Glancing at the screen, Rita did a quick search and then announced, "Yes."

"Finally," Dugan cried. He needed to get away from these two people before he lost his temper. "What room is she in?" he asked as he began to walk to the elevator.

"She's not," Dale called out after him. "She checked herself out yesterday."

# *Chapter Three*

"You're serious?" Dugan asked the attendants. This just wasn't adding up. "She just had a baby," he said. "Aren't you people supposed to keep them here for at least three days?"

"This isn't a prison, officer," Dale told him, obviously taking offense at the implication that they or the hospital had failed in some way. "Patients are free to go home at any time."

"What about the doctor?" Dugan asked. "Wouldn't he or she have ordered against something like that? And by the way, it's detective, not officer," he said, pointedly correcting the man.

"Well, *detective*," Dale said with an exaggerated bow of his head, "the doctor can make a recommendation, but if the patient chooses to disregard that

recommendation, the patient is free to just sign herself out and leave whenever she wants to. Unless, of
course, if she's being restrained," he added, glancing toward the woman beside him to make sure he
was right. Rita nodded. "But that's a whole different story."

"Bottom line, detective," Rita told him in a far
more polite voice than Dale was using, "the woman
you're looking for isn't here any longer."

Dugan blew out a breath, then shrugged. "Well, I
tried," he said, addressing his words to the woman.
He'd already used up the twenty minutes he'd allot-
ted himself. He needed to be getting to the precinct.
"That's all a man can do." Dugan offered her a smile.
"Thanks for your help."

And with that, he turned away and walked out of
the hospital lobby.

He had no doubt that the woman wasn't there anymore. There was no reason for either of the people,
even the irritating idiot, to have lied to him. What
bothered Dugan was *why* the woman from the other
night wasn't there any longer.

And why she had given him—or the hospital—
a phony name.

*Not your problem, Dugan,* he told himself as he
made his way back toward his car. *You gave it your
best shot, which is more than a lot of other guys
would have done. And apparently, for whatever reason, the woman had no desire to stick around longer
than she has to.*

Still, he had to admit as he crossed the lot, the detective in him was really curious about why someone like Scarlet—or whatever her real name was—would just leave the hospital so quickly after having given birth. The experience had to have exhausted her. Wasn't a stay at the hospital supposed to help her get back on her feet?

Maybe, Dugan thought as he finally reached his vehicle and got into it, it was just a simple matter of not having any insurance coverage. She couldn't pay her bill, so she gave them a phony name and decided to pull a disappearing act before anyone in the administration office had a chance to check her out.

But if that was the case, then why hadn't she tried to talk the hospital into letting her pay her bill off over time? People did that sort of thing. Sometimes the hospital would just write off a patient's charges.

"You've got a legitimate case to work on," he told himself out loud. "You don't have any time to try to figure this out."

Pushing the thought out of his mind, he started up his car. Puzzles were for people who had time on their hands to try to solve them. He, on the other hand, had a dead CI whose murder he was trying to solve. Someone obviously felt that Mitch Gomez had known too much and *that* was the mystery that took precedence over everything else, not some missing mama who had checked out of the hospital too early.

A missing mama with a gun, he reminded himself as he drove to the precinct.

When he'd first attempted to come to her aid, he recalled that the woman had tried to reach for a gun. Had she not been tied up in knots because of those contractions, he had no doubt that she probably would have shot him.

What—or who—was the woman afraid of? Dugan wondered.

"Later, damn it," he ordered himself sternly. "Think about this later. Not now."

The rest of the way to the precinct, he did the best he could to push all the other thoughts aside. He was a detective first, a man with a mystery woman to pursue second.

A *far* second he reminded himself.

The answer didn't satisfy him, but for now, it was going to have to do.

They were getting nowhere.

Eight weeks later they were no closer to finding out who had put that bullet into Mitch Gomez's head than they had been when the body was first found.

He and Jason had canvassed the area, talking to more people in the last two months than he probably had in the last six months, and still nothing. People talked, but in the long run, they said nothing.

Oh, he had a few suspicions about who might have been responsible—Michael Oren, a higher-up who represented the Juarez cartel in California—but suspicions had never won a case.

Not only that, but now he was currently down a partner, as well. Jason had broken his tibia and it looked as if he was going to be sidelined for the next few weeks if not longer.

"Tripping over your eighteen-month-old daughter, who *does* that?" Dugan demanded when he went to see Jason at his home to see how his partner was coming along.

"Apparently I do," the detective answered almost morosely. Fighting with his crutches, he managed to make it over to an easy chair. The whole adventure had left him exhausted. Three days and he still hadn't gotten the hang of maneuvering the crutches.

"I mean, she's not *that* tiny a baby. How could you have missed seeing her?" Dugan asked, shaking his head.

"Believe me, when you're not looking for an eighteen-month-old baby, they're easy enough to miss—and trip over," Jason grumbled.

His mother-in-law, who was babysitting the little girl, looked as if she was less than thrilled to also act as a part-time nurse for Jason. The look on his face showed that he felt the same way.

Jason lowered his voice so that only Dugan heard him. "Look, I'm sorry that this leaves you high and dry right now. I should be able to get around with crutches pretty soon."

Dugan had seen Jason attempting to maneuver into the room. He didn't hold out much hope.

"Right," Dugan replied sarcastically. "Just do me a favor. Stay home and get well. Fast," he underscored.

Jason glanced over toward his mother-in-law. "As fast as I can, trust me," he responded.

"I'll check back with you in a few days," Dugan promised.

And with that, he left.

Dugan had some thinking to do, and right now, he was better doing it alone. Granted, he and Jason had been a team for the last year and a half, but now that Jason was home for what looked to be some time, for now he was on his own in this investigation. He was *not* about to tackle the investigation *and* break in a new partner.

Granted, he could walk and chew gum at the same time, but at the moment, all his energy was concentrated on unraveling the massive drug connections that were involved here.

Factions of the Juarez Cartel had brought their territory fight against the Sinaloa Cartel up here. He didn't have time for anything else. Besides, he'd worked alone before and he was more than willing to do it again. It was definitely preferable to putting up with a new partner. Besides, if he needed backup, there were always Patterson and Ryan to call in.

His mind was made up. Until things changed, he was going to be working alone.

"Cavanaugh, get in here," Lieutenant Jerry Daniels called out the moment Dugan walked back into the Vice squad room.

He didn't like the sound of that, Dugan thought. But he couldn't very well pretend not to have heard the lieutenant and walk out again, not when he was certain that the man had seen him come in.

With a sigh, he braced himself and then walked into the lieutenant's office.

"You wanted to see me, sir?" he asked.

The words dribbled out of his mouth. He was aware of her the moment he walked in and was doing his best not to stare.

Even though she had her back to him, the tall, stately blonde sitting in the other chair would have been hard to miss. He could only hope that the woman didn't have anything to do with his assignment. Maybe she was involved in some kind of a goodwill gesture on the lieutenant's part, or—

She turned around to look at him. Recognition was immediate.

"It's you."

Dugan hadn't even realized that he'd said the words out loud until the lieutenant looked at him, obviously curious.

"You two know each other?" the lieutenant asked uncertainly.

There was no sign of recognition on the woman's face whatsoever. Either she was one hell of a poker player or she was the victim of a sudden case of amnesia, because it was her, the woman in the alley. He would have known her anywhere. She was the woman he'd helped to give birth…

If he stood here and insisted that he had been there eight weeks ago, hovering over her in that back alley, coaching her as she pushed out her baby daughter, and she didn't say anything to back him up, he was going to come across like a complete idiot who was on his way to a nervous breakdown.

So, for now, he was going to deny that he knew her—or how.

"No, my mistake, sir," Dugan said formally. "I thought I recognized your guest here, but I obviously don't."

Daniels nodded, accepting the explanation. "All right, then. If you're through interrupting me, we can get on with this. Since your partner is temporarily out on medical leave and the two of you weren't getting anywhere in your investigation anyway," he said crisply, his words cutting like a knife, "I thought that maybe another angle in this investigation might prove useful."

He was getting that feeling again, Dugan thought. That feeling where the back of his neck began to prickle, getting itchy. It happened every time that he felt something was going wrong.

He told himself he was overreacting.

"And what angle might that be, sir?" he asked in the calmest, most virtuous voice he could summon, even though he could feel his stomach beginning to tie itself up in knots.

The look that Daniels shot him told Dugan that his superior thought his tone was a little too innocent. But because there was someone else in the room and he wanted to come off at his best, Daniels was forced to keep his temper.

So, instead, Daniels just continued with his introduction. "That would be where Ms. O'Keefe would come in."

"Ms. O'Keefe," Dugan repeated. Was that finally

her real name or was this just another alias? At this point, he couldn't be sure. "That would be you?" he asked the woman sitting in the other chair.

The woman smiled at him. The smile was polite, distant and showed absolutely no sign of any sort of recognition in any manner, shape or form.

Leaning forward, she extended her hand to him and introduced herself.

"Toni O'Keefe, investigative journalist," she told him in case he thought she was part of the police department.

Dugan never took his eyes off hers. "Detective Dugan Cavanaugh."

"Pleased to meet you, Detective Cavanaugh," Toni said, still smiling that impenetrable smile.

Daniels looked from his detective to the extremely attractive woman in his office. It was obvious that he seemed to be trying to understand if there was something going on here other than just an exchange of introductions.

"Ms. O'Keefe, it turns out, is an expert on the history and dealings of the Juarez drug cartel," Daniels told him.

"Is that a fact?" Dugan said, pretending that this piece of information was actually interesting to him. "I'm sure it must make for fascinating reading, but right now, I think figuring out what their next move is might be a little more to the point than reading about where they've been."

He began to get up, but the look on the lieutenant's face had him silently taking his seat again.

"Sorry about that," the lieutenant apologized to Toni.

Her smile in return was brighter than sunshine. "No offense taken, lieutenant."

It became clear to Dugan that the lieutenant was attempting to cull favor with the woman.

"Ms. O'Keefe's father was Anthony O'Keefe," Daniels told Dugan. The name meant nothing to Dugan, but the lieutenant went on as if it should. "There wasn't a place in the world that journalist wouldn't go to, a lead he wouldn't chase down. He was fearless—"

Dugan was feeling restless and he had no idea just what his part—if any—was in this exchange. "I'm sure he was, lieutenant," he finally said, gripping the armrests as he got up for a second time, "but I have got work to do—"

That was when the lieutenant hit him with a line he really wasn't expecting. "And you'll do it with Ms. O'Keefe."

Dugan looked at Daniels, dumbfounded. While it was true that the lieutenant wasn't at the top of his field, he wasn't exactly an idiot, either. What was the man doing?

"Excuse me, sir?"

Everything in the rule book said that police work was done by members of the police department. Nowhere did it say that they were to defer to a newshound, or whatever it was that this person wanted to call herself—if she was even who she said she was. He was beginning to have his doubts.

There was one thing he did know. "She's not a police officer, sir." He looked at Daniels, waiting for the man to relent his position.

"She's anything I say she is," Daniels retorted, angry at what he felt was a challenge to his authority. "And right now, she has the clearance to be here and to help us in our investigation, so until such time as I decide it's no longer beneficial to this department, she is going to be working with you. Have I made myself clear, Detective Cavanaugh?"

"Perfectly," Dugan replied, doing his best to remain civil rather than to challenge the man.

It wouldn't do him any good anyway. The lieutenant, for reasons he could only begin to guess at, had made up his mind about including Toni O'Keefe in the case. He'd never been all that close to Daniels, who had only been heading up Vice for the last nine months, so maybe there was something he didn't know about the man—or this woman, for that matter.

For all he knew, maybe the lieutenant was the father of that baby she'd just had two months ago. Dugan was vaguely aware of the fact that the man was married, but that sort of thing might not have mattered to Daniels in this case.

At any rate, he was not about to waste time trying to figure out what was going on.

Instead, he was just going to get out of here and ditch this woman, whatever her game was, the first chance he got.

"All right," Daniels was saying. "Are there any

questions you might have for me?" He was looking directly at the journalist when he asked the question.

On an absolute basis, Dugan could see why the lieutenant might be acting the way he was. The woman, whoever she really was, was a stunner now that he actually looked at her. There was no other word for it. At approximately five foot seven, with long dark-blond hair and eyes the color of the sky at midday, she was gorgeous enough to catch anyone's attention and make them forget everything, including the end of their sentence.

But they weren't just "anyone," they were members of the police department, and as such, they had a duty to perform, one that came before everything else. Or so he liked to believe.

Didn't matter. All that mattered now was to get out of this room and get on with what he'd been about to do when the lieutenant had called him in. Granted, he wasn't getting anywhere with his investigation, but he hadn't given up yet. He certainly wasn't going to get anywhere by following around a so-called newshound, no matter what Daniels wanted him to do.

"Just one," Toni said, her voice sounding remarkably like Marilyn Monroe for someone who wanted to be taken seriously.

"And what's that?" Daniels asked, turning almost into a schoolboy right before his eyes.

"What do I do about Detective—Cavanaugh, is it?" she asked, looking at Dugan with wide eyes.

Before he could answer her, she had turned her

attention back to the lieutenant and continued, "If he suddenly decides to ditch me and take off?"

"He won't do that," Daniels answered. "Because there would be consequences to pay if he did that and he knows it." The lieutenant looked at Dugan pointedly. "Right, Cavanaugh?"

"Right, sir."

"Well, then, I guess we'll get out of your hair and get started," she said brightly.

"Remember," Daniels said to her as he ushered her out of his office. "Any trouble at all, please don't hesitate to get back to me."

"Oh, I won't," she told him. Then, looking directly at Dugan, she smiled as she added, "As a matter of fact, Lieutenant Daniels, you can count on it."

# Chapter Four

The moment he was out of the lieutenant's office, Dugan headed straight for the outer doorway leading out of the squad room. He had no particular destination in mind, other than to get away from the woman he had just been saddled with.

But if he'd meant to leave her behind, he found that she had other ideas about that.

The moment he stopped by the elevator to push the down button, she was right beside him.

He decided to ignore her. But that was before she said what she said.

"You didn't come to the hospital the way you said you would."

That stopped him cold. Turning to look at her, he saw a completely different expression on her face. It wasn't that vacant, cheerful look she'd worn in Daniels' office. The woman from the alley was back.

"Then you do remember."

"The most important night of my life?" she asked, surprised that he would think otherwise. "Yes, of course I remember. How could I forget?"

"Then why did you just act as if you didn't know me back there?" Dugan asked.

She looked around. For the moment, they were alone, so she explained her reasoning. "Because I wanted to do this story and I didn't think your lieutenant would have put us together if he thought we had a history."

Dugan didn't have to think about that. "You're right, he probably wouldn't have." Daniels tended to be the type who always had to be on top of everything, otherwise he was jealous.

Dugan got on the elevator. Toni was quick to follow. He moved back, giving her space—although part of him didn't want to. The thought of getting closer was extremely appealing. "But we don't *have* a history," he pointed out, pressing for the first floor. "We had about forty minutes together in less than perfect circumstances—Scarlet."

The elevator doors closed. They were alone but that could change at any moment. She talked quickly. "It's not Scarlet," she told him.

"I already know that," he said, annoyed. There was no point in raising any recriminations. But he did want to know one thing. "Why did you lie to me?"

That was simple enough. "Because I didn't know

you from Adam and for all I knew, you weren't a cop the way you said you were."

He supposed that was fair enough. He thought of something else. "And that gun on the passenger seat, that was for protection?"

She nodded. "Yes."

"Midnight's kind of a strange time to be out joyriding," he told her, skeptically.

"I wasn't joyriding," she informed him. "I was driving myself to the hospital. The baby decided she didn't want to wait any longer and was earlier than anticipated."

They had arrived on the ground floor, but he didn't get out right away. "Why didn't the baby's father drive you?" he asked.

Toni walked passed him, getting out of the elevator. "I think you've used up your allotment of free questions for the time being," she told him.

"One more question," he said, holding up his index finger. "What's your *real* name?"

So he thought she was lying to the lieutenant. She supposed she had that coming. Besides, even if she was lying, if he was the detective she thought he was, it wouldn't have taken him much to find out the truth.

"It's Toni. Toni O'Keefe, just like your lieutenant said," she answered.

"And just what are you supposed to do?" he asked. "Shadow my every step while I collect intel and try not to get shot by anyone associated with the drug cartels?"

They were in the police station lobby and the person at the reception desk was looking over at them, obviously curious. Toni ignored him.

"You've already asked your one question, but I'm feeling magnanimous so, yes, that's the general idea."

Dugan frowned. That was just stupid seven ways from sundown, he thought. "And whose bright idea was it for you to play Lois Lane?"

She raised her chin. "Mine." He started walking, so she quickly fell into place beside him. Or tried to.

"Does this mean that you think you're Clark Kent?" she asked.

"Hell, no." He laughed at the idea. "If I'm going to *be* anybody, it'd be Superman."

She smiled at him. "Okay, Superman, where do we go first?"

She could smile all she wanted to, but he wasn't some idiot to be led around by the nose by a beautiful woman. "We're not going anywhere until you explain to me *why* I would take you with me."

"Because your boss said so," Toni answered innocently.

Too innocently as far as he was concerned. "Not good enough," he told her. "I answer to a higher boss than Daniels."

Okay, so he was one of those, she thought. Someone who felt he had a connection to another, out-of-this-world power. "Oh, you mean like—"

"The chief of detectives," Dugan told her before she could make a guess. "Who also happens to be my uncle, but don't let that get in your way."

She'd seen that look before on other people. He was digging in and he wasn't about to give an inch until she convinced him otherwise. Luckily, this was not her first encounter with a man like this.

"Look, can we go somewhere for a cup of coffee and talk?" she asked him.

"We could," he said in a voice that told her he wasn't about to.

She made a quick decision. Leading the way out of the lobby to the police parking lot, she said, "What if I told you that that night you came to my aid, I had the gun with me because I was afraid someone from the cartel was after me?"

"I'd say you were really reaching." Although, he had to admit, he wasn't dismissing what she'd just said altogether.

"Then you'd be wrong," she informed him flatly, daring him to say otherwise.

He did a quick calculation. "Okay, let's go get that cup of coffee and you see if you can convince me I'm wrong," he told her, adding, "I'll drive."

"Fine with me." They'd gone down the back stairs and were at the edge of the lot. "Is that your car?" she asked, pointing toward the red Mustang one row over.

"Yes." He hadn't been in his car that night when he'd come across her. He'd left the Mustang parked a block away. Dugan look at her quizzically. "How did you know?"

"I remember passing it that night on my way to the hospital. Just how much do you get as a vice detective, exactly?" Toni asked as she stopped by the car.

He wasn't sure what was going through her head, but he didn't want her laboring under any misconceptions. "I rebuilt this car before I ever joined the force," he told her.

"You did this yourself?" she asked, clearly impressed with the end result of his efforts.

"Took me three years." He opened the doors. "Why?"

"And it runs?" she asked.

"Yes, it runs," he answered. "I didn't push it here. Why all the questions?"

"Sorry, occupational habit," she told him. She got into the car. "But if I had a car like this, I certainly wouldn't risk driving it around on the job. Don't people shoot at you?"

"Hardly ever," he told her.

That didn't make sense. "Doesn't Vice attract bad guys?"

She was getting sidetracked, he thought. "You want to go get that cup of coffee and convince me why I should let you come watch me for a couple of days or not?"

"The former," she told him.

Nodding, he started the car. "By the way, how's the baby?"

She looked at him, and for the first time, he saw a wary look in her eyes. "Why?"

"No reason. I helped bring her into the world—" he began.

"Technically," she said, cutting him off.

"And *technically*," he continued, "I'd just like to know how she's doing."

Toni looked straight ahead of her at the scenery, her expression impassive. "She's fine."

Dugan glanced at her profile. "Aren't you supposed to be with her?"

"What *is* it with you and all these questions?" she asked. "I'm supposed to be the investigative reporter here, not you."

He shrugged. "I just like to know who I'm going to be working with—*if* I'm going to be working with you," he qualified.

Sighing, Toni looked up at the roof of the car, as if seeking some sort of guidance. "I'm Toni O'Keefe. I write for the *San Francisco Times* as well as several online blogs. My father was Anthony O'Keefe and he taught me everything I needed to know about what it takes to be a good reporter. He taught me not to give up until I had my story and I never have." She looked at him now. "I don't intend to start now."

"Fair enough," he answered.

Dugan drove to the next block and pulled into an strip mall. It had an upscale grocery store on one end and a hardware store on the other. The coffee shop, along with a couple of other small restaurants as well as a pizzeria, were in the middle. He parked his car close by and got out.

"Best coffee in the city," he told her once they reached the coffee shop. He gestured for her to go in first.

After getting their coffees, he took her over to a

small indoor table. It was only when she sat down that he asked, "What if I don't want you to work with me?"

She didn't even hesitate. It was as if she was expecting this question, even though there had been a seven-minute break in between her statement and his.

"It'll take me longer to get my story," she informed him, her eyes meeting his. "But I'll still get it."

She seemed sure of herself, he'd give her that. "And if I let you work with me, exactly what is it that you bring to the table besides a great pair of legs?"

"I know people who you would want to know. People who could be very helpful to you. People who *know* things," she told him. "On their own, what they know doesn't amount to very much. But you start to put it all together, you just might have something."

She was dealing in suppositions and possibilities, Dugan thought. It could all be just a bunch of nothing. But she had guts and a certain style he found himself admiring.

Just as he was about to tell her that he'd take her on—on a trial basis, she surprised him by asking, "You think I have great legs?"

Ah, vanity, you had to love it. "Absolutely. They're probably the best pair of legs I've seen in a long, long time," he said.

"Oh." Realizing that she'd allowed herself to be distracted for a moment, Toni murmured, "Thank you." Then she turned her attention back to what they had been talking about. Clearing her throat, she asked him, "So, do we have a deal?"

He was silent for a moment and it was very obvious that he was looking at her legs. After a moment, Toni drew them farther under the table, shifting so that they were now on the other side of the chair rather than closer to him.

Raising his eyes to her face, he said, "I'll give you a week, see where it goes. But the first minute I find that it's not working, or you've done something to jeopardize the operation, it's over."

"You have an operation?" Toni asked, leaning forward as if she expected him to let her in on a secret. He saw interest flash in her eyes. She seemed to come alive right in front of him. "What is it?" she asked.

"All in due time, O'Keefe," he told her evasively. "You'll find out all in due time."

She watched him for a long moment, as if she was trying to discern just what it was that he had. And then she gave him a knowing look.

"You don't have anything. You're just doing this by the seat of your pants, winging it, if you will." Having caught him, she still wanted verification. "I'm right, aren't I?"

"Now who's asking too many questions?" Dugan countered.

"I *am* right," she declared. "That's okay. There's no shame in winging it. Some of the best plans are the ones that people have come up with on the fly," Toni told him with a smugness he should have found irritating—but didn't.

"Were you always an annoying little girl or did you grow into the role?" he asked.

She grinned and he found it annoyingly endearing. He was going to have to be careful around this one.

"I guess I've been like this my whole life," she told him.

"Huh. Remind me to send your mother a condolence card," he told her flippantly.

He saw her face cloud over for a moment. "That might prove hard to do," Toni said as she finished her coffee.

He indicated the cup with his eyes. "Refill?" he asked.

"No, I'm good," she answered.

Dugan heard the distance in her voice. Ordinarily, that would have been enough to make him back off, but for some reason, it didn't. Instead, he returned to his previous comment about sending her mother condolences. Her expression had changed at that point, he thought. What had he said wrong?

"Why would that be hard to do?" he asked. "Send your mother a condolence card," he prompted when she said nothing.

She thought about getting up and walking out. She also thought about telling him it was none of his damn business. Neither option really worked for her. At the very least, neither would get her what she wanted and she wanted that story. A huge drug bust as it was happening.

So she told him the truth.

"She died when I was born. She insisted on being

with my father while he went after stories no one else would. She had the bad luck of being one of those women who didn't look pregnant when she was, so nobody told her she shouldn't fly late in the pregnancy." Her voice was almost robotic, as if she was reciting a narrative that belonged to someone else. "She went into labor on the flight home. There were complications. She didn't make it. At least Dad was with her when she—didn't make it," she concluded in a voice that was far too cheerful for the subject she was narrating.

Tossing her head, she asked him, "So, do I really get to work with you, like you said, or are you going to make my life more complicated by making me shadow you for every piece of information I want?"

For just a moment, Dugan understood what she was going through and what she had to be feeling. "My mother died, too."

Her eyes narrowed. "That's not what I asked you," she informed him almost coldly.

He didn't know if she was trying to push him away or if he had managed to embarrass her somehow just now by cracking a wall he hadn't realized she had up around her. For that matter, he reminded himself, he really didn't know if she was on the level. For all he knew, she could have just made that whole thing up to get on his good side *because* she knew that his mother had died when he was young and highly impressionable. After all, his life wasn't exactly a secret.

"No," he replied, his eyes on hers. "It isn't."

"So do I?" she asked him again. "Do I get to work with you for a week while you make up your mind whether or not having me around is beneficial to your trying to break up the Juarez drug cartel?" she asked him again.

"And if I said no, you really would wind up shadowing me?" he asked.

There was no hesitation on her part. "Yes," she answered.

"Well, then, I'd better save us both some grief and just say yes," he told her. "Temporarily," he added before she could say anything to either thank him— or tell him that he had made a wise choice.

Either way, he felt he had no other option. And he had learned a long time ago that it was better to have the source of his problem with him at all times than somewhere behind him.

There was less chance of being shot that way.

# Chapter Five

"This is what you have?" Toni asked, looking at the bulletin board.

They had returned to the precinct and were now in the Vice squad room. There were close to a dozen photographs pinned to the bulletin board, arranged in a staggered tier formation, with the current head of the Juarez Cartel in the US located at the top.

All the photographs were of men. In addition, there were a few sheets of white eight-by-ten paper posted amid the photographs. These blank sheets represented the key figures in the organization who had *not* been identified, men within the cartel in different positions of importance who were able to make things happen, to have shipments sent out or received, but hadn't been named.

Yet.

Whether this was because they were so important that their names were kept secret, or because the people who *had* been questioned previously didn't know their names was unclear to Toni at the moment.

"This represents over eighteen months of work," Dugan told her. It had taken that much time and effort—and more—to compile these names and faces.

"And these?" Toni asked, tapping one of the empty pages. "How long did it take you to put *these* up on the board?"

Unfazed, Dugan told her, "Those represent works in progress. The people exist, we just don't know their names yet. We thought perhaps we were getting close to finding out some of their identities, but our latest CI turned up floating in a lake just around the time you gave birth," he said grimly. "The one before that disappeared off the face of the earth." He sighed. "We'll probably find him in a shallow grave sometime in the future. The life expectancy of a CI who's associated with this particular cartel isn't exactly what you might call long."

"Maybe that other CI you mentioned decided that it was healthier for him not to play both sides against the middle and just disappeared," Toni guessed.

But Dugan shook his head. "Even when they stop giving us information, it's only a matter of time before something gives them away to a superior. The cartel has a lot in common with a school of piranha. If they have nothing to feed on, they turn on their own. The trick is not to give them a reason to feed on you," he said.

Toni shivered and ran her hands up and down her arms. "Makes you wonder why anyone would ever get into that way of life."

He considered her question. "Other than stupidity, for some it's the promise of money. A great deal of money," he underscored. "For others, it's an easy pipeline—at least at first—to something that they think that they can't live without."

She could see supposed informants clamming up, refusing to talk to the police. She tried to understand how any of the Vice detectives ever managed to get anyone to volunteer any actual information.

"Given that, how would you hope to be able to cultivate a CI?" she asked.

That was simple enough from where he was standing. "Some people are smart enough to realize that they're standing in quicksand and they feel that making a deal with us—i.e., trading us information for a reduced sentence, or at times no sentence at all, is their only hope of keeping out of jail."

Toni eyed him rather skeptically. "And you let them believe that?"

Dugan frowned slightly. He didn't see a problem with the method and rather resented her insinuation that he was lying.

"We *let* them believe that because it's true. We're their last hope," he told her. "At least we won't put a bullet in their heads," he added.

"Not directly, anyway," she countered.

His eyes narrowed as he regarded her. "What's that supposed to mean?"

"Didn't you say that your last CI won't be making any more reports about possible shipments because he wound up going for a swim he hadn't counted on—with a bullet in his brain?"

Dugan became a little wary. "I didn't tell you that," he said.

"Sorry," she apologized offhandedly. "Must have been in the report I read."

"That happened on the day you gave birth," he said. "That was the phone call I got so I couldn't go to the hospital with you," he told Toni, looking at her. "How did you...?"

Toni shrugged, passing it off. "Like I said, I must have read it," she admitted. "I've been boning up on the cartel," she reminded him. "I didn't want to come to the party empty-handed."

"So far, you're only offering me leftovers," he told her, far from pleased at the way this investigation—and her part in it—was going. He still didn't see an advantage to having her working with him. As a matter of fact, he could see it going the other way very quickly. To his way of thinking, journalists were not known for their caution.

She nodded, taking in what he had just said. "Then I guess I should tell my people to get busy and bring me something you can use."

That caught him off guard. "What people?" he asked.

"People-people," she answered.

He gave her a skeptical look. "You're going to have to do better than that."

But this time, she wasn't about to try to win him over. She became serious. "Sorry, Cavanaugh. You know I can't give up my sources or else they won't give it up to me. All I can do is pass whatever I get on to you when I get it," she told him.

This made him think that the woman had seen one procedural too many. She obviously thought this was a game. He had no patience with games.

"Look, any tip we get, we're going to have to vet," he told her.

Rather than back off, the way he thought she would, or just give up altogether, Toni said, "Then I guess it's going to be a long time between tips, at least on my end." She pressed her lips together for a moment, choosing her words carefully. "Look, how about if I promise that whatever I do pass on to you is legitimate? I'm not about to do it for brownie points, Cavanaugh. If what I give you turns out to be bogus, I know that you'd dump me."

Dugan never hesitated. "In a heartbeat."

That only proved what she was saying. "I know that, you know that, so there won't be any phony leads just for the sake of leads."

Dugan felt his patience beginning to slowly evaporate. He sighed. "So, after all that, do you have anything?"

He still half expected her to lie. Instead, she spread her hands wide. "No, not right now. But you'll be the first to know when I do."

He looked at her for a long moment, and then something occurred to him. "These leads that you get…" he began.

"Yes?"

He watched her expression the entire time as he asked, "Do they have anything to do with that gun you had on the passenger seat that night?"

The wide smile she'd had up until that moment faded. A serious expression came into her eyes. The whole tone of the discussion changed.

"They might have," she told him guardedly.

"Anything you want to talk about?" he asked her, waiting for her to give him something to work with.

Instead, she said, "No."

He tried another line of questioning. "Are you still carrying that gun?"

Dugan saw her raising her chin defiantly. He had his answer before she said another word. "I have a permit."

"So I take it that's a yes?" Whether or not she said anything, he knew that it was.

There was silence between them for a moment. And then Toni changed the subject. "Why don't you tell me what you plan to do next with this investigation?"

He had questions he wanted to ask her. Questions that had to do with why she was doing something so ultimately dangerous when there were so many other things she could be writing about. Questions about why someone as savvy as she seemed to be would have gotten herself into a situation where she had wound up trusting the wrong man, as she obviously must have done, given the fact that he'd found her in an alley, about to give birth, instead of somewhere with her husband or boyfriend being taken care of.

Questions filled Dugan's head that had absolutely nothing to do with why she was standing here beside him right now.

But she *was* standing here with him right now and he had to deal with that first and everything else, no matter how curious it made him, second.

He forced himself to focus on the case he'd been working on for over eighteen months. "We round up the people caught in the most recent drug busts and talk to them to see if they'd heard anything about the next shipment."

"Just like that?" Toni asked him incredulously. Was he that naive?

"Well, I might be leaving out a couple of steps," Dugan granted. "Like maybe their little brother or sister was picked up on drug charges, too. And maybe we could make that go away. Or make their second possession with intent to sell be knocked down to a misdemeanor if they have anything to trade."

All right, now he was talking, Toni thought. It was beginning to make sense to her. "Do you have anything like that?"

"I'd have to check my roster," he told her, unwilling to say yes or no. He continued looking at her for a moment, then he shook his head. "Do you realize that you're about to salivate?"

Rather than be embarrassed or say that he was imagining things, she boldly told him, "Just looking forward to seeing you in action, Cavanaugh."

His smile was slow, making her heart flutter once it was out in full force. "Well, if that's the case," he told her, "maybe we can see what we can do about that after my shift's over."

Just for the slightest second, there was a zap of electricity that traveled between them. She could hardly move. But then she rallied, backing away—gracefully, she hoped.

"Sorry, I have a baby to see to once I'm through here."

He was wondering when she would get around to mentioning the baby. He'd started to think that maybe she'd given the baby to someone to watch over while she was on this assignment. She certainly didn't act like any new mother he'd ever come across.

"Maybe I could drop by to see her," he said, inviting himself over without a hint of embarrassment. "She's got to be what, two months old now?"

Toni had to admit that he'd surprised her. Most men didn't keep track of anything but their favorite team's standing in whatever league they were in. When it came to anything else—babies, occasions, the women they'd gone out with—their minds were, for the most part, blank slates.

This made him different, she thought.

"Two months," Toni repeated with a nod, then almost as an afterthought, added, "Maybe someday," regarding his request to see the baby.

"Sure," he answered. "Just name the day, I'll be there."

Okay, she had to ask. "You're serious," Toni said, more in wonder than to confirm what he'd just said.

"Sure," he answered. He didn't understand her question. "Why wouldn't I be?"

She thought of her daughter's father. The moment he had found out that she was pregnant—and that she wasn't about to terminate the pregnancy—he had dropped out of the picture completely. He'd made it clear that he preferred not to know anything about the details, including if she'd had a girl or boy or a cockatiel. As far as he was concerned, they'd never even been together. She hadn't heard from him in almost a year.

"Most men aren't interested in babies," she finally said.

To her surprise, Dugan laughed, then really laughed. Not at her, but at her statement.

"What's so funny?"

He'd almost had tears in his eyes. Taking a deep breath to steady himself, he said, "I was just thinking that I was going to have to introduce you to the men in my family."

*Right, like that's going to happen,* she thought. The only time men talked was when they talked about women.

"Let's start out with something simple," she told Dugan, changing the subject for the second time in less than half an hour. "Like one of those drug arrests you mentioned."

There was more to her than just being an annoying investigative journalist, he thought. There were layers to this woman. Layers he was going to enjoy peeling back when the time came.

But for now, she was right. His case had been stalled for over a week and it was time to shake a few trees and see what fell out.

"Okay," he told her, writing down a couple of things in a very battered notebook he took out of his pocket, "Let's get to it."


"I need a hit, man," the jittery woman told Dugan.

Scrawny and unkempt, she looked older than her years. She had long since stopped caring if her hair was combed and her makeup was on correctly or even at all. A one-time picture of perfection, now Linda Tanner only cared about finding her next score and the sooner she found it, the better.

Her window of comfort had come and gone and she was desperate now. A ring of perspiration circled her hairline and she was rocking in her seat as she talked to him, as if the perpetual motion would somehow help soothe her.

It didn't.

"You wouldn't have anything on you, would you?" she asked. She knew he didn't, but she was hoping against hope anyway. Hazel eyes darted toward the woman sitting beside the cop. "How about you? You have anything? I just need a taste, just a little taste, that's all. I'm going crazy here," she told Dugan, her attention shifting back to him since he was the one she knew. Her fingertips turned almost pale as she dug them into his arm. "C'mon. *Please*," she begged, looking from one to the other. "Just a little taste to see me through."

Toni had seen junkies before, some up close and personal, like this one. But there was something about this woman that seemed to hit closer to home than the others.

Toni shifted uncomfortably, looking at Dugan. They were sitting opposite the woman in a communal room at the city jail.

Toni turned her head so that only he could hear her. "Can't you do something for her?" she asked.

"Are you suggesting that I get her drugs?" Dugan asked, wondering just what it was that she wanted him to actually do.

"I'm suggesting that you do something to help her get past this point. Something to tide her over," Toni said. Otherwise, all they'd hear was her lamenting her situation.

"Is that what you want, Linda?" Dugan asked, looking at the wild-eyed young woman. "You want something to tide you over?"

"Yes," she cried, saying the word with such emphasis her eyes looked as if they were about to pop out of her head if she squeezed them any more.

Toni wasn't sure what to expect. Part of her thought he'd tell the woman no. Instead, she heard Dugan say, "You know the game, Linda. You have to give me something to get something."

Toni looked at him. Then he *was* going to give the woman something?

He'd done this before, she realized. It made him no better than some of the people he was looking to put away, but she supposed there was some sort of justification for what he was doing. In his place, she wasn't sure just what she would do, especially if she had something in her possession to give to the woman.

"I don't have anything to tell you!" Linda cried, desperate.

"Think, Linda," Dugan said calmly, his voice a direct contrast to hers. "You haven't heard of anything going down? No shipments supposedly coming in now or at a later date?"

"Later, maybe," Linda said, her eyes really wild now as she seemed to struggle to think. "Later," she repeated. "Out of Baja," she added. "The fifteenth of next month. Maybe the twentieth." She licked her lips as she scratched her arms. She continued scratching, all but taking the skin off.

"Is it a small shipment?" Dugan asked.

She shook her head, her matted head moving like a separate entity about her head. "No, not small. Large. I overheard them. They said it was a large shipment." Her breathing grew a little more shallow. Whether it was the excitement of what she was saying or the idea that she was going to get something to alleviate the awful craving she was experiencing wasn't clear. "When they saw me, they stopped talking, but I heard what I heard," she maintained.

"I'm going to have to check it out, Linda," Dugan said.

"I'm not lying," Linda cried. "You know me. *Please*," she begged. "You said if I told you something, you'd get me something."

"And I will," he told her.

There were tears in her eyes as she clutched his arm. "Now!

# Chapter Six

"Linda, listen to me carefully," Dugan said, getting in close to the woman and articulating every word slowly. "I need to know where and when this shipment is coming in," he told her in the same calm voice he'd been using.

Rather than answering, Linda let loose with an exasperated scream that sounded as if it had come out of a much larger woman. Then, just as the police officer began to hurry over toward their table to subdue her if necessary, Linda said, "All right, all right."

Dugan raised his hand and waved the police officer back. He never took his eyes off Linda.

"I'm waiting," he told her.

Linda slanted a look toward the woman beside

Dugan. It was obvious that trust was very much of an issue for the heroin addict.

"This is just for your ears only," Linda told him.

He glanced at Toni. "Would you mind?" he asked. His tone told her that it didn't matter if she did or not, he needed to have her walk away for the time being.

Toni wasn't happy about it, but there was nothing she could do, so she got up from the table and walked over to the far side of the room. Only then, when she was satisfied that she wouldn't be overheard, did Linda lean into Dugan and give him the information he was asking for.

Finished, Linda straightened up again. "Okay?" she asked, a performer eager for evaluation. "Can I get my hit now?"

Dugan beckoned the police officer forward. "Give her what we talked about earlier, Seth," he told the officer.

The vagueness of Dugan's response disturbed the woman. "I'm getting a hit, right?" Linda asked. "You promised. You said—" Taking her arm, the officer began to lead her away.

"You'll get your hit," Dugan told her as the woman was taken out of the communal room.

Toni stared at him, stunned. "You're actually having them give her drugs?"

"Methadone," Dugan told Toni once he was sure that the woman was completely out of earshot. "She's going to get methadone." Getting up, he walked out of the room, turning toward the doors that eventually led to the outside world. "I talked to the doctor here and she's being started on a methadone program to slowly get her off heroin. The methadone will ease her pain, although she's definitely not going to get the high she was hoping for."

Once outside the jail, he looked at Toni. "Still want to cover this story?" he asked her. "You were turning an interesting shade of green back there for a couple of minutes."

She supposed that she owed him an apology— but he could have warned her about this beforehand. "That was when I thought you were going to contribute to her drug habit."

He didn't bother hiding his smile. "I thought you said you did research on this."

They were back in his car now and Toni felt uncomfortable. She looked straight ahead through the windshield rather that at him. "I did."

"I'd say that your research was a little shoddy, O'Keefe. Otherwise you'd know that all things considered, I might not always do things a hundred percent by the book." Since he wasn't going anywhere yet, he looked at her as he spoke. "But I always stay on the right side of the law that I'm supposed to be defending."

"Sorry," she murmured. And then she finally looked at him. "I didn't mean to insult you."

"I'm not insulted," he said. "I was just misrepresented and maligned." Humor played along his lips and he smiled at her, magnanimous at the moment. "I'll let it slide this time."

She wasn't sure how to play this, so she went with

a touch of humor. "Do I genuflect, or will a simple thank-you do?"

"The latter'll do," he said. "As long as you lose the attitude."

Toni began to protest his assessment. "I don't—" But it was obvious that he was right. She actually *did* have an attitude. She wasn't being fair. So far, he'd been pretty decent about this and even if he hadn't been, she knew she owed him for what he'd done for her in that alley two months ago.

She blew out a breath. "Okay, you're right. I'll lose the attitude."

He finally started up his car, heading back to the precinct, which was close by. "As far as I can tell, I've treated you rather fairly considering that the lieutenant sprang you on me without any warning."

A few choice words rose up, but she squashed them. "You did," she grudgingly admitted.

He nodded. Apparently they were in agreement on their assessment of the situation. But he still needed to clear something up.

"So would you mind telling me why you're acting as if you're expecting me to leave you standing on the side of the road in the desert at any second?"

A denial rose to her lips, but she could tell that he would see beyond that and they both knew it. She might as well not waste his time. So she decided to do something novel. She went with the truth.

"Because I've been fighting to be taken seriously ever since I could remember and I learned that striking the first blow is much better than being taken by surprise by a sneak attack and being caught with your defenses down."

"That's an old tune," he said dismissively.

"Doesn't mean it doesn't ring true. Look at me," she told him. She held out her hands, as if they somehow blocked his view of her. "Everyone thinks I get things handed to me because of my looks and that they're going to be the one who doesn't cave in and follow the pattern.

"The problem is, there *is* no pattern," she insisted. "Nobody hands me anything because of my looks. I have had to fight for everything ever since I decided to be like my dad—and my fight started out with my dad," she told him. "Except with him, he didn't want me doing this because he didn't think it was safe, flying around the world, doing stories about the world's underbelly."

Eventually, he'd changed his mind and been proud of her, but it had been a hard-won victory that didn't last all that long. He died shortly afterward. But she still savored the memory.

"Like about the drug cartel," Dugan guessed.

She knew what her father would have had to say about the story she was pursuing now. Toni shrugged. "Like about the drug cartel."

He was silent for a moment, as if rethinking his assessment. And then he nodded.

"Okay, why don't we both start over?" he suggested. Then, before she could ask him just what he meant by that, he stuck his hand out and said, "Hi, my name's Detective Dugan Cavanaugh. And you are…?"

"Going to laugh at you," Toni answered, doing just that.

"Going-to-laugh-at-you," he repeated, being completely serious. "That's a rather unusual name. Is it Irish?"

Toni found herself laughing again, more heartily this time.

"Okay. You've proved your point. We start fresh," she agreed. "So," she said after taking a breath and wiping tears away from her eyes, "where do we go from here? How do we find out if that woman's so-called *tip* is on the level? Or are you just going to follow that lead?" she asked. "I take it that this woman gave you some information when you granted her that private audience she'd asked for."

"Actually," he told her, "It was just more of the same." He saw her looking at him skeptically, but he didn't say anything further to make her change her mind. "I'm going to have some of the team that's working the streets put the word out to their people, see if anyone else's CI can confirm—or deny—this information."

"So we sit back and just wait?" she asked him in disbelief.

"No, we go out and gather more information from the usual suspects, the small-time wheelers and dealers who are just buying enough to keep their own habit going. On any given day, there are any number of deals going down, drugs changing hands for payment. We are going to hit some of the usual spots, see if we can find anyone who feels like talking."

"You're kidding, right?" she asked as he finally started up his car.

"Why don't you tell me what you really think?" Dugan told her with a straight face.

"I think that riding around with you, Detective Cavanaugh," she told him, making sure her seat belt was on, "is going to be a once in a lifetime experience."

He grinned. "Oh, well, now you're just trying to flatter me," he told her, pulling out of the lot and into the street.

"So," she asked as they left after questioning yet another junkie, "How did I do?"

Dugan spared her a quick glance before he turned his attention back to the road. His expression gave nothing away. "You need practice."

She settled back in her seat and looked straight ahead. "You'd be the first one to say that," she told him with a smile that was completely unreadable.

It made Dugan think nonetheless. Think and, just for a moment, allow his imagination to run away with him. But these were working hours and he was working, so for now, any thoughts he had beyond that were going to have to be tabled.

But there would come a time, Dugan silently promised himself, when he would find the chance to explore those thoughts and follow them to their natural conclusion.

That made him smile.

* * *

"Want to stop by Malone's?" Dugan asked several hours later back at the police station.

The endless day had finally ended—unproductively as far as she was concerned, although she did have several colorful things to include in her series once she wrote it up.

But for now, she was completely wiped out and quietly praying that her daughter would allow her to catch a couple of hours of sleep before Heather woke up, demanding her attention. That was all she really needed to be able to get back on her feet, Toni thought, just a couple of hours.

However, a couple of hours was her rock-bottom minimum.

"Malone's?" she repeated now, realizing that he was waiting for an answer from her. The name meant nothing to her. She put her notebook into her purse and waited for Dugan to continue.

He obliged with an explanation, although it was hard for him to imagine that there was someone who didn't know what Malone's was. The bar was a very active presence in his life as well as the lives of everyone around him. It was where the people at the precinct came to let off steam and just center themselves.

"That's a local bar where cops hang out when they're not on duty." He'd suggested it because he got the impression that she was looking to do the "whole" cop experience, and Malone's was definitely part of that. "It's also the place I was coming from that night I ran into you," he added, deciding to frame the incident as delicately as he could.

They needed to get past that night, Toni thought. It gave him far too much of an intimate advantage over her. She wanted to be on equal footing with him and having Cavanaugh recalling that incident put her in his debt.

"Ah, well, thanks, but no thanks," she told him. Then, not wanting to rule it out completely—after all, things could change—she quickly added, "Some other time maybe. But right now, I'm really bushed and I have a baby to go home to." She paused as she double-checked her purse for her car keys and fished them out. "Lucinda probably wants to go out."

"Lucinda." He rolled the name over in his head. "Is that what you named her?"

She looked at him, confused. "No, she came with a name."

It was his turn to be confused. "What?"

About to leave the squad room, Toni pulled up short, rethinking what had just been said. "Wait, you're talking about the baby, aren't you?"

Of course he was. And then he looked at her, confused. "Aren't you?"

Now it was starting to make sense. "No, I'm talking about the nanny I hired to take care of my baby while I'm at work."

He started at the beginning again. "What's the *kid's* name? Your daughter," he added for good measure, just in case her nanny still qualified as a kid.

"Heather." Toni started to tell him the baby's mid-

dle name, then realized that would be a mistake—
because it was his name—so she just stopped dead
before she said it. She didn't want him feeling that the
name connected them more than it did. "Heather,"
she repeated.

Dugan nodded his head. "Heather," he echoed.
"Nice name."

"Glad you approve." Toni pressed her lips together, stopping herself cold. "Sorry," she apologized. "That was flippant. I didn't mean that the
way it came out sounding."

He looked at her, mildly curious. "How did you
mean it?"

"I didn't mean it in any particular way at all," she
told him. "Being flippant is a tough habit to break,"
she admitted.

He grinned and his expression caught her completely by surprise. She felt herself melting just a
little.

That would have to stop. Melting had been what
had gotten her into trouble to begin with—if Heather
could be called trouble, she amended, thinking of
her daughter.

"You get points for trying," he told her. "So, I
guess I'll see you tomorrow—unless you decide to
change your mind and write about something more
mainstream."

"What's more mainstream than drugs?" she asked
with a laugh.

"Offhand, I could name a ton of things," Dugan
answered.

She supposed that was true. "I'm sure you could—and they've all been done to death."

"So have articles on drugs," Dugan pointed out.

"Mine will have a new perspective."

He sincerely doubted that, but it was the tail end of the day and he wasn't in the mood to spend another hour of it arguing with her, which was what would happen if he contradicted her in any manner, shape or form. It was better to pretend he hadn't heard her and just continue on his way.

"I'm sure it will," he said with as straight a face as he could manage, and then he walked out of the squad room.

"You didn't mean that, did you?" she asked as she hurried after him and joined him in the hallway.

He looked at her as if he didn't know what she was talking about.

"I was agreeing with you," he insisted.

"But you didn't mean it, did you?" Toni pressed again.

"You're like a pit bull with a bone, aren't you?" he asked her. And then he sighed. "I said it because I wanted to leave here. You have somewhere to be and I have a mug of beer calling to me, so why don't we just smile, say good-night and let everything else go for tonight?" he suggested as they got on the elevator.

She still wanted him to answer her. "But—"

"I promise that if you still want to argue about the meaning of any statements tomorrow morning, I'll be here, bright and shiny, ready to go a couple of rounds with you, if you want."

"Bright and shiny?" she repeated, doing her best not to laugh.

"Best description I can come up with right now. I'm tired. I do better when I'm not tired," he told her. "Just take the win and go."

"There's no win," Toni pointed out, bemused at his choice of words.

"Okay, a placeholder for a win, how's that?" he asked her. "Look, we can both agree that it's been a long day, right?"

"Right," she began tentatively, but got no further.

"And that we're both tired, right?"

There definitely was no arguing with that. She couldn't remember being this tired—or this wired—for a long time. "Right."

"So let's do as I said. We stop now and pick this up in the morning—if that's what you want to do in the morning," he qualified.

She shook her head, really confused now. "You're going around in circles."

He smiled. They had reached the first floor. He got out, not waiting for her. His best chance, Dugan decided, was to just keep going and make it out the door.

"And with that," he threw over his shoulder, "I bid you adieu."

# Chapter Seven

"I'm home, Lucinda! Sorry I'm late," Toni called out as she unlocked the front door and let herself into her house. Closing the door behind her, she quickly rearmed the security system.

"That's okay. I love hanging out with your baby." Lucinda, a small, slender young woman with straight black hair and warm brown eyes entered the living room almost at the same time that Toni walked in. Her sharp eyes missed nothing as they skimmed over the older woman. "You look kind of tired, Toni," Lucinda noted. "Did you have a hard day?"

Toni smiled ruefully. While she would have denied it had anyone else asked, she saw no reason to pretend around Lucinda. Theirs was a relationship built on trust and it had taken her some time to build that up.

"I am," Toni admitted. "It's been a while since I've put in an actual full day." She dropped her purse on the sofa. "I couldn't *wait* to get back and get my feet wet again, but I think I need to pace myself a little more until I recapture my momentum."

"Don't worry. I'll stay overnight," Lucinda told her. It wasn't an offer but a statement. "That way you get to catch up on your sleep. Besides, your place is a lot nicer than mine is."

"No," Toni said, turning her down. "I can't let you do that. I can't let myself fall back into bad habits like that."

"Catching up on your sleep is *not* a bad habit," Lucinda told her. "And trust me, I'm an expert on bad habits. You're still a new mother and you need to build up your strength."

Toni realized her mistake. She really was tired or she wouldn't have allowed her protest to slip out the way that it had, at least, not worded that way. "I didn't mean to make it sound as if you—"

Lucinda cut her off with a wave of her hand. "I know you didn't. You've been nothing but good to me, Toni." Her expression softened a little as she remembered. "You took me in when my own family threw me out and slammed the door in my face."

She was not about to let Lucinda to feel bad about herself. "They didn't mean to do what they did, Lucy. Your family was just frustrated that they couldn't find a way to help you."

Lucinda smiled, resigned. "You can make up all the excuses you want for them, but you and I both know the truth. I had a drug habit and they didn't want to deal with it, so they just pretended it—and I—didn't exist. I don't know where I'd be if you hadn't made me go to that rehab clinic and then gave me a job once I got out." She'd been Toni's assistant until the baby came and then she had gone on to become Heather's nanny. "Most likely I'd be dead," she concluded grimly.

"No, you wouldn't." Toni slipped her arm around the young woman. "You're a fighter, Lucy, and you know that you don't owe me anything," Toni told her with feeling.

"You're wrong there," Lucinda replied. "I owe you everything." Clearing her throat, she said, "Now, I've got some soup for you on the stove. After you have that, I want you to go to bed."

"But it's still early," Toni protested, although not with much energy.

"Doesn't matter. You need to get some sleep," Lucinda insisted. "And don't worry about Heather. I'll be here to take care of her."

"But I just said you don't have to stay the night," Toni reminded the younger woman.

Lucinda shook her head. "And I told you that I don't care what you said. I'm staying—unless you want to throw me out."

"Lucy, you know that I wouldn't do that—" Toni began, still trying to get the young woman to change her mind.

Lucida cut her off. "Good, so it's settled. You eat your dinner, then go to bed." She was about to say something else, but she stopped abruptly, listening. And then she smiled. "I think your daughter's decided that it's time to see if Mommy's come home yet."

Toni gave it one more try, albeit a halfhearted one. "You know you don't have to do this, Lucy."

"Sure I do," Lucinda contradicted, her small, heart-shaped face lighting up. "Doing these little things makes me feel useful. And happy."

She'd hardly call them little things, Toni thought. What Lucinda was doing was tantamount to saving her life. "Thank you."

"Don't mention it. Seriously, don't mention it," Lucinda insisted. "Now if you don't mind, the baby needs my attention. I'll bring her out once I'm done changing her," she added.

Even if Lucinda was staying the night, Toni did want to see her daughter before she went to bed. "You are a mind reader," Toni marveled.

"One of my many talents," Lucinda said, leaving the room.

Toni turned her attention to the pot on the stove in her kitchen. She knew that she should have put up more of a fight about taking care of the baby and sending Lucinda home, but the truth of it was, she did feel utterly exhausted. So exhausted that she didn't even know if she could finish eating the soup that Lucinda had prepared for her. All she really wanted to do was close her eyes and go to sleep.

Taking a bowlful now, Toni made her way over

to the table and sat down. She had no sooner put a spoon into the soup than Lucinda came in with the baby.

Lucinda had grown up taking care of three younger siblings. She'd forgotten how fast the young woman could be.

"See? There she is," Lucinda told the bundle in her arms. "Told you Mama was home."

Forgetting all about her dinner, Toni rose from the table and took the tiny bundle into her arms. Love swelled all through her.

"Hi, baby. I missed you today," she said softly to Heather. "Did you grow very much since I left this morning?"

"Boy, you are tired, Mama," Lucinda said in a high-pitched voice, pretending to answer as the baby. "Babies don't grow in just ten hours—unless they're baby tadpoles. Now eat your dinner and go to bed so that you can grow up big and strong, like me."

Toni laughed and paused to kiss the baby's soft, downy head before she handed the infant over to Lucinda. "Okay, Heather. Don't give Lucinda too much trouble."

"Naw. Me and Lucy are pals. Now go to bed." Lucinda stopped for a second and looked at her over the baby's head. "Really, the second you finish eating, go to bed. That's an order. From both of us," she added.

"I'm paying you to take care of Heather," Toni reminded the younger woman. "Not me."

Lucinda shrugged. "Consider it a twofer. Just accept it and stop giving me grief," she ordered.

There was a hint of a smile on the nanny's lips as she left the room.

"You're too good to me," Toni called after Lucinda's departing back.

Lucinda never stopped walking, but she did manage to say, "Right back at you," before she went into the baby's room.

Toni could barely finished eating. Taking the bowl to the sink, she rinsed it out, then started to make her way up the stairs. She was halfway there when she stopped. The one thing she knew she needed to do, no matter what else she allowed to let go, was make sure the security system was back up and armed. She was fairly sure that she had rearmed it when she came home, but it didn't hurt to double-check, just in case.

Going back to the front door, she told herself that she was being paranoid, but she truly believed in the old "better safe than sorry" adage. After all, she thought with a weary smile, just because you were paranoid didn't mean that they weren't out to get you. And she was dealing with some really bad people, taking on this story. She knew that.

Lucinda was the reason she'd gotten caught up in this drug cartel story to begin with. Lucinda and people like Lucinda who got caught up in the drug trade and became casualties of the ensuing drug wars.

Not because they were looking to profit from selling drugs, but because they—Lucy and people like her—were the ones the drugs were sold to. People whose futures were lost because they became slaves to the opiates they were taking, and when those were no longer available to them turned to heroin to appease their cravings.

And died along the way, Toni thought angrily.

She didn't have any illusions. She knew perfectly well that she couldn't stop the flow of drugs, not by herself and most likely not even with the help of an army of people, but at least she could dam up the flow from one pipeline—if she was lucky.

Toni entered her room. She didn't bother turning on the light. Instead, she just made her way to her bed.

Damming up the pipeline was the last thought that crossed her mind before Toni fell, face down, onto her bed.

After that, she didn't remember a thing.


"So, ready to tell Daniels that you're fed up and you're not going to work with that fine young woman he saddled you with?" Adam Henderson asked, slipping into a seat right beside Dugan.

Five months away from retiring, the Vice detective was strictly old school—the way school had been more than two decades ago. He also seemed to know a lot about everybody else's business around him.

Dugan had never much cared for the man and he didn't particularly like the fact that Henderson relished sticking his nose into everyone else's affairs, but he kept that to himself.

"No, not yet," Dugan answered. "I thought I'd stick it out a little while, see what she has to offer."

Henderson chuckled, his grin positively wicked as he said, "I can tell you what she has to offer."

Dugan felt himself getting defensive on Toni's behalf even though he hardly knew her. Henderson's grin rubbed him the wrong way. "No, not like that."

"Why not like that?" Henderson asked, stunned. "You're letting a perfectly good morsel go to waste." He shook his head in almost disgust. "You know what's wrong with all you Cavanaugh boys?" the older detective asked. Putting down his mug of beer on the table, he sloshed a little over the sides. It dripped onto the table.

Apparently Henderson wasn't about to go away until he had some feedback, so Dugan decided to play along—for now.

"No, enlighten me," Dugan replied. "What's wrong with us Cavanaugh boys?"

Henderson looked as if he was more than happy to tell him. Settling in, the slightly overweight detective said, "You're too honorable and squeaky clean. To get the job done, you need to get down and dirty, get in the trenches and take care of business the way it should be taken care of," he declared.

Picking up his mug again, he took a big gulp, his movements a little sloppier now than they had been a few moments ago. He seemed to be feeling his beer and obviously enjoying the trip.

"Maybe you should stop now," Dugan suggested tactfully. "You've had enough to drink."

Henderson looked at him as if he had lost his mind. "Hell, no, I've got a whole night ahead of me.

I'm just getting started, son," the detective declared with a laugh.

Rather than argue with him, Dugan looked toward the front of the room. He saw one of the owners tending the bar and he signaled to him, trying to catch the man's eye.

One look in his direction and the tall, almost hulking former police officer behind the counter came forward, weaving his way around the tables to theirs. At six-six, few men even thought to argue with Kyle Denver.

"I'm cutting you off, Henderson," Kyle told him, his deep voice rumbling from within the depths of his barrel chest.

Dark, bushy eyebrows drew together, forming an angry, wavy line as Henderson looked up. "You can't do that," the inebriated detective protested.

"I own the bar. I pour the drinks. I can do whatever the hell I want," Kyle said, patiently contradicting the other man. Turning toward the bar, he signaled someone at the far end. A slightly smaller version of Kyle came quickly to attention. "Cal, call our satisfied customer here a cab. He's going home."

Henderson rose on shaky legs. He almost pitched forward, then caught himself at the last moment, grabbing the back of a chair to steady himself.

"The hell I am. I'll go home when I'm good and ready to go home!" Henderson announced.

"Adam—" Dugan began, attempting to persuade the other man to leave the bar as quietly as possible without a fight.

But Henderson had other ideas. In response to the sound of Dugan's voice, Henderson swung around, fist ready and made contact with Dugan's face before the latter could duck out of the way.

Recovering, Dugan quickly caught Henderson's arm, bent it behind his back and instantly brought him down to his knees.

"He's ready," Dugan told the owner over Henderson's angry cursing.

"Thanks, I'll take it from here," Kyle told him, taking possession of Henderson. "By the way, your tab's on me," he told Dugan just before he herded a very indignant Henderson away.

"That is definitely *not* going to look pretty tomorrow," Duffy Cavanaugh judged. Dugan's younger brother sat down in the chair that Henderson had just unwillingly vacated. Cocking his head to take a closer look at the damaged area, he told Dugan, "However, if you ask me, it might actually be an improvement."

Dugan turned to his brother. Younger by eleven months, Duffy was two inches taller, making him the tallest one in the family. Dugan looked accusingly at the younger man.

"Where were you?" he asked.

Duffy jerked his thumb back toward the far side of the room. "Over there, watching. I figured that you didn't want your little brother to come running to your rescue." He eyed Dugan innocently. "Was I wrong?"

Dugan didn't have an overblown ego that caused him to believe he could win every fight that came his way.

"I might have been able to use the help." He ran his hand gingerly along his face just beneath his eye. The sharp pain caused him to wince. "He sucker punched me."

Duffy nodded. "Yeah, go with that. I would."

"It's true," Dugan informed his brother indignantly.

Duffy grinned. "I didn't say it wasn't," he told Dugan. "What was he carrying on about, anyway?"

Dugan put the whole story in a nutshell. "Daniels stuck me with a reporter."

Duffy rolled the words over in his mind, nodding. "Sounds interesting. Is she cute? Better yet," he said, not giving his brother a chance to answer, "Can she help? You know, like with inside information or coming up with some source that no one else thought to tap into?" Unlike Henderson, Duffy, like the rest of his extensive family, was a cop first, a man second.

Dugan paused. He looked his brother up and down before saying anything. "Honestly?"

"No, lie to me," Duffy cracked. "Of course, honestly."

"It's still too soon to tell," Dugan answered, and then he let his brother in on his thoughts. "But I'm thinking that this had to clear the chief of Ds' desk, right?"

Duffy immediately knew what his brother was

thinking. "And he wouldn't have given his okay in the matter if she was just some cute piece of window dressing. By the way, is she?"

"Is she what?"

"A cute piece of window dressing," Duffy repeated. "Keep up, son."

Dugan grinned. "You know, I've got a good mind to let her know you asked that, just to get back at you for *not* coming to my aid."

"You haven't answered my question," Duffy reminded him.

"No, I haven't," Dugan said, putting down his mug and getting up. "But, just so you know, there's no law that says she can't be both. Cute and competent," he specified just in case his brother had lost the thread of the conversation.

"Okay, now I want an introduction," Duffy told him brightly.

"Too bad," Dugan said, beginning to walk away. "Because you're not getting one."

"Hey, Mom told you to be nice to me, remember?" Duffy reminded him.

"No, she didn't," Dugan answered as continued walking toward the front of the bar and the exit.

"Okay, then I'm asking you to be nice to me," Duffy said, never missing a beat.

"I am," Dugan said, glancing over his shoulder just before he walked out of the bar. "I'm not punching you for not coming to my aid."

Duffy had followed him to the door. "That doesn't count."

"It does to me."

He heard Duffy laughing in the background. Dugan grinned to himself as he went out.

## Chapter Eight

Dugan arrived at the station earlier than normal, thinking that he'd get some work done before his babysitting detail officially began. But when he walked into the squad room at a quarter of eight that morning, the woman who had been assigned to him was already there. Holding court, as it were.

The detectives who were already there for one reason or another were obviously drawn to her. They surrounded the desk she was temporarily occupying—Jason Nguyen's desk, because it was unoccupied for the time being.

As Dugan walked by, he heard her asking the other detectives questions, jotting down their answers and in general apparently ingratiating herself with each and every one of them.

If he thought, because she was holding court, that he'd be able to get to his desk unnoticed, he found himself disappointed. The moment he had passed by her desk, Toni stopped interviewing the others. She thanked everyone for their candid answers to her questions and then, with two containers in her hands, she walked over to his desk.

"'Morning, Cavanaugh. I brought you coffee," she told him, indicating one of the containers she was holding.

He saw the insignia on the side of the cup. The coffee had come from one of those shops that specialized in high-priced, foamy coffees that went for slightly less than a pound of coffee beans.

"I don't drink fancy coffees," he informed her. He knew that wasn't the trend, but he'd never been one to go along with the popular trends unless they suited him. "I prefer to take my coffee black."

"Yes," she said, taking the lid off the container to show Dugan the opaque liquid that was inside of the cup. "I know."

He looked at the journalist quizzically. "How did you—"

Toni smiled. "I watched you. You had coffee yesterday. Three times," she recalled. "Each cup was blacker than the inside of an old-fashioned inkwell," she told him. "The barista was disappointed when I ordered your coffee this morning, but on the plus side, he didn't have to do anything to the coffee after he poured it." She smiled, backing away. "The one I ordered for me, of course, made up for it."

"Thanks," Dugan murmured. Taking the coffee container from her, he took a giant sip. And then another one. Only then did he nod toward the crowd that was just dispersing. Some of the detectives were still looking her way. "By the way, what was all that about?"

About to have some of her coffee, Toni paused. "All what?"

"That," he repeated, this time swirling his finger around to indicate her desk and the detectives who had been gathered around it.

"Oh, that." Toni shrugged casually. "I was just spitballing, asking questions to gather information for possible future articles."

"Huh." He turned that over in his mind for half a second. A thought occurred to him. He had a glimmer of hope as he asked her, "Maybe you'd rather go with one of them. I wouldn't be insulted," he added quickly, trying to be encouraging.

He'd had a full night to think about this situation and he had come full circle, back to his initial position of not really wanting her tagging along if he could possibly help it. He didn't want to be responsible for her.

"But I would," Toni told him, then asked, "Are you trying to get rid of me, Cavanaugh? After all the nice things I wrote about you?"

"What nice things?" he asked, mystified. "And just where did you write them?" He regarded her rather skeptically. Had she already put something down in writing? Where? And, more importantly, would it jeopardize his operation?

Toni laughed. "Relax, Cavanaugh. I was speaking hypothetically. I haven't really written anything yet—except in my head. And I won't write anything," she added quickly, "until after you get who you're after. I know the drill."

"Then maybe you'd better not plan on writing anything for a long time," he warned her. "This operation could be over tomorrow—or, more likely, in another year."

"The first estimate is way too soon," she told him. "But the second one is too pessimistic. I have faith in you, Cavanaugh. You're the kind who gets whatever he's after—and sooner than later."

He looked at her for a long moment, trying to decide if she was just talking and pulling his leg or if she actually had looked into his work. If it was the latter, he wasn't used to that. He was the one who did the investigating, not the other way around.

"Just exactly how much *do* you know about me?" he asked.

"Enough," was her vague answer. "Tell you what, if you're worried, I won't publish anything until you take a look at it and okay it for publication."

She wasn't about to win him over that easily. "How do I know you won't go back on your word?"

"Ah, well, that's where the trust part comes in. I'm trusting you to be honest with me—and you're going to have to trust me."

Right now, he trusted her about as far as he could

throw her and he had a feeling she knew that. But he was also saddled with her until she decided to call it a day—or the lieutenant decided that he didn't want to make nice with the press any longer.

Whatever else Dugan had been about to say on the matter was momentarily tabled when one of the other members of the Juarez Cartel task force looked into the room to deliver a message.

"Hey, Cavanaugh, word is that Michael Oren was just spotted at the Eastmount Town Center Mall, just outside of Oakland. First actual sighting in a while," the detective, Harry Everett, announced, pleased to be the bearer of good news. Oren was currently considered to be the number two man in the cartel since they had undergone restructuring last year. "This might be your only chance to get to him. Who knows, you might even wind up turning him," Everett said needlessly.

Dugan didn't need anything more. He was on his feet, pulling on his jacket. Moving quickly, he didn't even realize that he wasn't alone until he got to the elevator and another hand reached out to push the down button.

He looked at Toni, surprised. "Where do you think you're going?"

Her expression was innocent. She looked unclear as to why he was even asking her something like that. "With you."

When the elevator didn't arrive, he pushed the button himself, annoyed. "You do realize that this is dangerous. That if this turns ugly, there very well might be bullets flying."

Dugan waited, part of him expecting the journalist to back down. Whatever her job had been, she was a mother now and there was more to consider than there had been before.

Toni merely nodded as she slung her purse strap over her shoulder.

"I know," she told him. "I signed all the papers saying I understood what I was getting into and that I absolved the police force of all blame and liability if I should get hurt—or killed," she added so casually, he thought he'd misheard her for a moment.

The elevator arrived, but he put his hand in the way, blocking her passage. "This isn't some movie, Toni. These are the type of people you spend your life trying to avoid."

She raised her chin almost defiantly. But her expression remained the same. "You don't."

"I'm a cop," Dugan pointed out. "That means I can't afford the luxury of ignoring them."

"And I'm a journalist," she countered. "It's my job to expose these kinds of things so that our kids'll stay safe."

He was beginning to believe that she really meant those words she was saying, but that still didn't change the bottom line. This was dangerous for her, especially up close.

"Can't you do that from a safe distance?" he asked.

"Not nearly as effective," she told him. "Besides,

I'm not worried." She flashed him a smile. "I have you to protect me."

"And if something happens to me?" he asked. His point was that if anything happened to him, she'd be dead—or worse—in less than a heartbeat. He really didn't want her out in the field with him. But there was nothing he could do about it right now—except to get her to change her mind about tagging along.

And that wasn't going well.

"Tell you what," Toni suggested. "We'll protect each other."

He tried again. "Look, this isn't a game," he told her roughly. "People die dealing with the wrong person every day."

She looked up into his eyes. She wasn't nervous, he realized. Her gaze was unwavering. "I know that," she said in a quiet, firm voice.

He wanted to leave her here, at the precinct, where she was safe. He really did. But he had an uneasy feeling that if he tried to make her stay, she'd still follow him. In another vehicle, if she had to.

He decided that his best bet was to have her come with him and hopefully get scared enough to leave on her own.

"Okay, c'mon," he told her, then added, "Maybe you'll come in handy."

Dugan had her attention. "Care to elaborate on that?"

An idea came to him. It wasn't one he was going to put into action, but she didn't know that. Maybe this was what he needed in order to scare her away.

"Oren likes blondes," he told her. "Maybe he'll see you and be attracted."

"I'm bait?" Toni asked as she got into the car. He didn't know if she was horrified or just incredulous—but he had hope.

"You want to bail?" he asked innocently as they pulled out of the lot.

"Hell, no," she told him. And just like that, his hopes were dashed.

As a matter of fact, he could have sworn that she sounded as if she was actually looking forward to the experience.

Didn't the woman even have the sense she was born with?

"Don't get too excited, he might fly the coop altogether before we get there," Dugan told her darkly, annoyed that his plan to have her beat a hasty retreat had backfired.

Toni grinned. He could have sworn her eyes were sparkling. "I'll try to contain my excitement," she told him.

They drove in silence for a few minutes. Unable to take it any longer, Dugan finally had to ask and satisfy his curiosity.

"Why the hell would you volunteer for an assignment like this?"

Toni read between the lines. "Are you asking me why I'm not writing about something more appealing, like the new fall line or a juicy tidbit about the latest popular celebrity, or maybe about an exciting island getaway? Or, better yet, some article about puppies and what to do with them."

She was ridiculing him because she thought he was undermining what she did for a living. He got that. But it still didn't answer his initial question.

"No, not those topics—exactly—but, well, something a little less threatening and life endangering than an article about bringing down a drug cartel."

"Series of articles," she corrected, as if that was the only thing wrong with what he'd said and what she was ultimately doing.

"All right, *series* of articles," he ground out. When he looked at her, he saw that her expression was serious now. The cheerful young woman who had gotten into his car was temporarily gone.

"Because celebrities, island getaways, fall lines and puppies don't generally ruin people's lives," she told him. "Drugs do. Drugs can rob people of their futures, possibly their very lives. And for every addict that succumbs to the power of drugs, not just that person, but their husbands, their wives, their children and their parents are affected. They *all* suffer." Her voice took on a certain power he hadn't heard from her previously, not even when he was helping her deliver her baby. "Drug addiction and its consequences are a miserable scourge that destroys whole families, and if my article winds up saving just one person—and their family—then I've done something really good with my life."

Her impassioned words had caught him completely off guard. He looked at her now. "You really feel that way?" he asked.

"Those were a lot of words to waste if I didn't," she told him. "So, yes, if there's any doubt left in your mind, I do feel that way." She paused for a moment, then because he wasn't saying anything, she said, "Anything else you want to ask me?"

"Who was it?"

She had no idea what he was talking about. "Who was what?"

"Who was it that you lost to drug addiction?" he asked.

She looked at him, puzzled. "Who says I lost anyone?"

"All right," he said, regrouping, "then who did you almost lose?" he asked. "Come on, you couldn't be this passionate about bringing down the drug cartel if this wasn't personal to you."

She shook her head. "Sorry to disappoint you, Cavanaugh, but maybe it's just a matter of me having a big heart. It could just be that I'm against drugs on a general principle."

She wasn't about to tell Dugan about Lucinda. That was Lucy's story to tell, if and when she wanted to tell it, not hers.

"Uh-huh."

His very tone told her that he wasn't buying her words. "What, you don't believe me?"

"Didn't say that," he answered loftily, moving back and forth through traffic, squeaking through lights before the traffic got too heavy.

"But you don't?" she guessed. His very body language gave Toni her answer.

He found that keeping her guessing was better than making an admission one way or another. "We'll see, Toni O'Keefe. We'll see."

They'd reached their destination and Dugan pulled up at the far end of mall. Getting out herself, she scanned the area.

It appeared to be an upscale mall, from what she could see, although it wasn't exactly what she was used to, but then, before Heather had come into her life, she'd traveled all around the globe, following stories from one locale to another and looking to see just where she ultimately fit in.

Eventually, she'd decided that her best fit was closer to home. She was familiar with it the way she wasn't with other places. And, ultimately, this was where she wanted to do some good.

"So where is he?" she asked Dugan.

Dugan's phone rang just then. He answered it rather than her. "Cavanaugh. Talk to me."

"I think you just missed him," Everett told him.

"You sure?" Dugan looked around. There were more cars parked in the area than a weekday warranted. "Where are you?"

"I'm at the south end of the mall," the voice on the other end of Dugan's cell said. "Oren just got into his car."

"Was he going left or right?" Dugan asked, looking around.

"He was going right."

"Maybe Oren just pulled over to the other side of the mall. You know, taking the lazy man's route instead of walking," Dugan told him. "It's safer that way. Was he alone when you saw him?"

"He was when I saw him, but there might be someone in the car," the other detective warned him. "I couldn't get a good look without giving myself away."

"Duly noted." Continuing to scan the area, Dugan stopped when he saw something familiar. "Hold it. Is Oren is still driving that dark blue Mercedes?"

"One and the same," Everett confirmed. "At least our guy's got some class. But I only got a partial plate."

"Partial is better than nothing. Give it to me," Dugan ordered.

"7JUU. He was moving too fast for me to get the rest," Everett apologized.

The man they were hunting had a habit of changing cars and switching out license plates, so this could very well not even be the car Oren was currently using, Dugan thought. However, a possible something was better than a definite nothing.

Dugan continued watching.

"I think I was right. Oren just pulled up on the north side of the mall." Dugan held his breath, waiting. "He's parking," Dugan told the other detective. "Now all we've got to do is see where he goes and close in on the bastard—without attracting any attention."

Standing next to him, Toni finally spoke up.

"School's out for a holiday today. The mall's bound to be full of students," she pointed out. "Won't surrounding the guy be kind of dangerous in these circumstances—to others, I mean?"

"I don't make the circumstances," he told her. Disregarding the journalist, he told the other detective, "Look, Everett, I'm going to see if I can get close to him. Stick close by. Maybe we can—"

Dugan stopped when he suddenly realized that Toni was no longer next to him by the car. Looking around, he scanned the immediate area, trying to locate her. "Where the hell did she go?"

"Where the hell did who go, Cavanaugh?" Everett asked.

"That journalist that the lieutenant wanted me to babysit. O'Keefe—"

And then he saw her. Toni had made her way across the parking lot and from where he was standing, it looked as if she was walking right toward Michael Oren.

"Oh, hell."

"What?" Everett demanded. "I'm flying blind, here, Cavanaugh. What's happening?" he asked. "Talk to me!"

Dugan blew out a breath. His first instinct was to run after Toni, but it was too late. And if Oren saw someone running in his direction, the man was liable to shoot first and ask questions later—if he even thought to do that at all before he barreled away in his souped-up vehicle.

"Lois Lane just went after her story," Dugan said angrily.

"What? English, Cavanaugh, speak English," Everett demanded. "Who's Lois Lane?"

"The journalist," Dugan said in disgust. "And I *am* speaking English."

"Then make sense, damn it," the other man cried, obviously confused.

"I only wish I could. The journalist just flew the coop and she's flapping her way over to Oren."

That caught the other detective's attention. "What the hell is she doing?"

Dugan sighed, recalling what he'd said to her just a few minutes earlier. "I think she's playing bait."

# Chapter Nine

Dugan couldn't get the image of a train wreck out of his head. Just like witnessing an actual train wreck, he was unable to look away. He also couldn't second-guess the outcome.

Although Toni was walking in Oren's direction, she appeared to be completely unaware of the man. Dugan held his breath. And just as she was about to pass Oren—which meant that she would actually be in the clear—he saw her suddenly trip, less than a foot away from the drug lord.

As he watched, he thought that Toni would actually fall flat on her face—and then, suddenly, Oren made a grab for her and caught her.

Damn it, Dugan thought, he should have put a bug on the woman right from the start just on principle.

\* \* \*

Toni's heart was pounding hard and she really didn't have to fake her distress. What she did have to fake was the expression of relief on her face when she looked at the man who had caught her. However, she thought she managed to carry it off rather well.

"Oh, I'm so sorry," she said, apologizing profusely and with just the right amount of embarrassment. She glanced ruefully down at her shoes. "These are new shoes and, to be honest, they're higher than I'm used to." She shook her head. "I should have never worn them to go shopping."

Oren finally released her shoulders. "On the contrary, they make your legs look extremely attractive." His dark eyes washed over her. "You should always wear high heels."

"Um, thank you." Toni cleared her throat self-consciously. "And thank you for catching me like that. Falling at your feet would have been really embarrassing."

Oren looked mildly amused. "It wouldn't have been the first time that has happened," he told her with a self-deprecating laugh. "Sorry, that was too much of a straight line to resist," he confessed. His command of the language, Toni caught herself thinking, was better than she'd thought it would be. "Can I give you a lift somewhere?" he asked her. "My car is right here. Or perhaps we could get something to eat?" he suggested.

"Oh, no, thank you. I'm meeting my mother in a few minutes," she explained quickly, as if she was trying not to insult him. "She's the kind of person who tends to panic if I don't show up when I said I would. I'm afraid that she's a little paranoid." And then she looked at him a bit hopefully. "Perhaps we could do that some other time?" she asked, leaving it up to him to agree.

"Sure. I'm busy tomorrow, but how is the day after tomorrow?" he asked. "Say around eight o'clock? There's a café not too far away from here. It serves the best Mexican food around. *Carla's*. Do you like Mexican food?" he asked her.

She had the feeling that he was dissecting her with his eyes.

"I love Mexican food," she told him with enthusiasm. "And I know just where that restaurant is," she assured the tall, darkly handsome man.

"Good. Then the day after tomorrow," he repeated. "Does eight o'clock work for you?"

"Eight o'clock is perfect." She glanced at her watch and frowned just a little. "But right now I've really got to go."

"Your mother," Oren said knowingly, nodding his head.

Toni flashed him a smile. "My mother," she confirmed. With that, she hurried off through the mall's double doors.

Dugan remained standing where he was, watching Oren as he watched the woman he had just met disappear into the mall. After a moment, Oren got into his vehicle and, less than a minute later, pulled out of the parking lot.

What the hell had just gone down? Dugan thought, shaking his head. He could feel himself growing angry. He sure as hell intended to find out.

As he started walking toward the mall's entrance, his cell phone rang. Expecting it to be Everett again, he pulled the phone out of his pocket and fairly barked into it.

"Cavanaugh!"

"You need to work on your telephone voice, Cavanaugh," he heard Toni tell him. "I know who you are."

"O'Keefe?" He looked around, expecting her to pop up near him. But he didn't see her. "Where are you?"

"I'm still in the mall. Has Oren gone yet?" she asked.

"Yes, he's gone," he told her. "He pulled out a minute ago, smiling like a coyote that's looking forward to his first bite of a tasty morsel. What the hell was all that?"

"I'll tell you everything when I see you," Toni answered.

The call terminated. The next moment, he saw her coming out through the large double glass doors again. Wanting to cut the distance and reach her, he made himself remain where he was, waiting for her to come to him, instead.

When she did, her face was flushed and she looked exceedingly happy with herself.

That made one of them, Dugan thought darkly.

"You want to explain what just happened?" he demanded the second she was at his side.

Toni smiled up at him brightly. "I have a date with Oren."

"You WHAT?" he cried, stunned.

Rather than explain out in the open, Toni got into the detective's car and waited for him to get in on the driver's side and join her.

The moment he did, she started talking. "You said that Oren liked blondes so I thought we could play up to his weakness. And it worked," she announced happily. "I'm meeting him at Carla's Café the day after tomorrow at eight o'clock. That's enough time for you to get your people in place and be ready, right?"

"Back up, Napoleon. Who said you could do this?" he asked, stunned that she'd taken this independent action on her own.

Toni looked surprised that he would even bring that up. "There wasn't enough time to ask for permission, Cavanaugh. Besides, if I did ask you, you would have said no."

"Damn straight I would have said no," he practically shouted. "Do you have *any* idea what you're doing?" he demanded. "This is dangerous and you're not a professional."

"I beg your pardon," she said icily, disappointed that he was taking this approach. "I'm an investigative journalist," she pointed out. "And this isn't my first rodeo." Her eyes narrowed as she looked at him. "I've gone undercover before."

He didn't care what she might have done before

this, although he had his doubts about any of her story. She was probably making it up as she went along. "Not on my watch you haven't."

"That would have been a little difficult to do, considering that I didn't even know you a few days ago." She took a breath, calming herself down and approaching this from another direction. "Look, it's a simple plan. I'll show up, Oren and I will have a drink, maybe even dinner, and just as his guard is down, you'll show up to take him prisoner. If something goes wrong before that, you'll be there to rescue me. I'm sure that you'll be watching his every move."

He didn't like the fact that she was so close to the truth. He would do it just this way *if* she were another police detective, which she wasn't. "Got it all worked out, don't you?"

"Not much to work out, really," Toni confessed with a quick shrug. "This just all fell into place almost by itself."

His eyes narrowed as he looked at her. "I don't like it."

"And I don't like eating broccoli. But it's supposed to do a lot of good for me in the long run," she retorted just as Dugan finally started up his vehicle.

He almost stopped the car at that point. Dugan shot her a dark, annoyed look. The woman was really messing up his thought process—along with other things. "What the hell is that supposed to even mean?" he demanded.

"Anything you want it to," she retorted. And then,

taking a breath, she calmed down and offered him a smile. "Look, as long as Oren shows up, one way or another, you can get him."

"I'm not comfortable with you taking chances like that."

For the briefest of moments, she couldn't help wondering if he was worried about her. Most likely, he was just worried about Oren getting away. If anything, she'd just be collateral damage.

"You didn't force me to do this," she reminded him. "It's my own choice.

"Look, O'Keefe," he said, his voice softening, "you have a new baby at home. You don't want to be taking these kinds of chances with your life."

"That's where you're wrong," Toni insisted. "It's because of my baby that I want to. Who knows how this will play out? Maybe what I wind up doing the day after tomorrow will somehow cut back the threat of drugs by just the smallest increment, which just might, in turn, keep Heather safe."

Dugan shook his head, at a loss as to how to get her to change her mind, or even how to reason with what she had just said.

Sighing, he said, "Well, I'm not going to argue with you anymore."

"But?" Toni asked. When he didn't say anything immediately, she explained, "There's a 'but' in your voice."

He laughed. "Maybe you are good at this kind of thing," he told her. "I'm not going to argue with you anymore, but I *am* going to run it by the chain of command. If they sign off on this thing of yours, we'll play it your way."

"Chain of command?" she echoed, surprised. She hadn't expected this much opposition to a spur-of-the-moment idea. "You're not going to let a perfectly good plan go because you're trying to keep me safe and it wasn't okayed by your people, are you?"

He rolled her words over in his mind. The truth of it was, if she were a police detective, he would have no problem going along with the plan, no questions asked. Maybe she *did* know what she was doing.

"All right," he said grudgingly. "This is against my better judgment but we'll do it your way. We'll wire you up—"

Her reaction was immediate. Putting her hand on his arm, she cautioned, "No wires." She saw that her protest didn't sit well with him and she was quick to explain her thinking. "Are you kidding me? Oren detects a wire, I'm dead where I stand."

"We've advanced," Dugan assured her. "The wire will be in your ring or your necklace. Maybe in your earrings. Nothing obvious. Besides, if you're not wired, you don't go. It's as simple as that," he told her flatly.

She looked at Dugan skeptically. "Are you sure this wire's undetectable?"

"Completely," Dugan promised. "We've got tech specialists whose sole job is to create listening devices that could catch the heartbeat of a hummingbird fifty yards away—without the hummingbird suspecting he's being listened to."

She looked at him doubtfully. He had to be putting her on. "How much of a market is there for that sort of thing?"

"Oh, you'd be surprised," Dugan assured her. "More than you could ever guess."

---

"The chief of detectives would like to see you," Dugan told Toni.

He'd disappeared the moment they returned to the precinct, only to return about ten minutes later to tell her that her presence was requested.

"The chief of detectives?" Toni repeated, surprised as well as suspicious. She didn't get up immediately. "Why?"

"Protocol," Dugan answered. Then, because she continued looking at him with those clear-water blue eyes of hers, those eyes that were getting right to him, he said, "The chief doesn't bite."

"I wasn't worried about that," she answered, following Dugan to the elevator. "I was just wondering what you said to him."

"The truth," Dugan answered. He pressed for the elevator. "He wanted to know how you were doing. The chief likes to keep his finger on the pulse of every operation that's going on."

She couldn't see how that was possible. Dugan had to be exaggerating.

"That must keep the man very busy," Toni commented drolly.

"He can handle it," Dugan said. The ride was quick. Quicker than she was happy about. And then they were getting out on the chief's floor. Dugan waited for her to join him. "You ready?"

"Lead the way—unless you're not included in this meeting you've arranged for me," Toni added.

His smile was wide—too wide, in her opinion. "Oh, I'm included."

She merely sighed as she continued walking to the chief of Ds' office. "I had a feeling you would be."

Chief of Detectives Brian Cavanaugh wasn't what she expected, and it must have shown in her face when she walked into his office and met him.

"Something wrong, Ms. O'Keefe?" he asked as he shook her hand, then gestured for her and Dugan to take the two chairs that were on the other side of his desk.

"No," she answered a bit too quickly. "Why do you ask?"

"Because you looked rather surprised when you came in just now," Brian answered. His warm gaze swift assessed the young woman. "Didn't Detective Cavanaugh tell you that I wanted to see you?"

"Yes, sir, he did," Toni answered, wondering how much, or how little, the man knew about her.

"Then…?" He left the rest of his statement up in the air, waiting for her to make a comment that would enlighten him.

"Very simply," Toni admitted, "You're not what I expected."

An amused smile slipped over Brian's lips. "And

just what was it that you expected?" the chief asked, curious.

She'd researched the principal people involved before she came to the precinct, but she hadn't included the chief of detectives. Toni was clearly surprised by what she saw.

"I was expecting someone craggy and old, I suppose. A man who was going to tell me that he wasn't about to put up with grandstanding or showboating."

"All good points," Brian agreed. "I don't usually have to say that, though, because none of my people feel inclined to participate in either behavior." His eyes were kind as they met hers. "They know better."

"I do, too," Toni informed the older, still quite vital man, refraining from slanting a glance toward Dugan.

Brian nodded. "Good to hear. But just to satisfy my curiosity, why *did* you feel you had to go off on your own to make contact with Oren? Why not wait for Detective Cavanaugh to set things in motion?"

"Well, sir," she began slowly, feeling her way around, "Detective Cavanaugh said that Oren liked blondes," Toni explained.

Brian smiled, nodding his head. "And you're a blonde."

"Yes, sir, I am," she said a little too quickly, and she was aware of it the second she said it. However, it was too late to backtrack, so she just forged ahead. "I just felt it gave me an in and I acted on it."

Brian nodded. "I appreciate initiative as much as the next man. More, possibly. But it is customary to check with the people you're working with *before* you go off to do something independently," Brian pointed out. "First and foremost, Ms. O'Keefe, we are police officers, not cowboys."

"You're benching me," Toni guessed, disappointed. He was doing it politely, but he was obviously going to teach her that acting independently had consequences.

Brian exchanged glances with his nephew before answering her. Toni could feel her stomach beginning to sink.

"Why would I do that?"

Toni blinked. "Excuse me? You're *not* benching me?"

"We've been trying to get Michael Oren or Manuel Hernandez, his superior, alone for several months now. They're the cartel's number two and number one men who are stateside at the moment," he interjected. "And you seem to have managed to corral Oren on your own in just two days. All qualifying ramifications aside, that's quite commendable."

She was still trying to make sure she understood what the chief was saying to her. "Then you're not telling me I can't go?"

"I'm encouraging it," Brian told her. "But the next time you get an idea in your head to go all Lone Ranger on us…"

She cut in before he could finish his sentence. "Don't," she guessed.

"No, but I want you to check with us first. At the very least," he pointed out, "you might have been stepping on the toes of another operation that was already in place."

That had never occurred to her. She looked at the chief now, wide-eyed. "I didn't do that, did I, sir?"

"Fortunately, no. But you might have," Brian repeated. "That's why, while you're here, I want you to run things by Detective Cavanaugh before doing anything. He might have an annoying trait or two," Brian allowed with a tolerant smile. "But he is quite good at what he does. And, more importantly, he'll make sure that you live to tell about this—or at least write about it—once it's all over.

"Now, all that being said, if you should wake up tomorrow morning and find that you've changed your mind about going through with this—"

"I won't," she told him firmly.

"—the option will be yours," he concluded. "All right, you two, that's it for now. But feel free to come back to see me if you have any questions or any doubts," he underscored. "Understood?"

"Understood," Toni promised.

With that, Toni left the chief's office. Dugan was right beside her.

## Chapter Ten

The rest of the day was filled with following up on other possible leads regarding the buying and selling of drugs, most of which could be considered as small-time.

For the most part, the day was a blur to Toni as the full import of what she had set in motion began to sink in.

On the one hand, she felt that she'd done something good and possibly brought the capture of one of the leading drug dealers a little closer to fruition. On the other hand, she felt that she might have started something that just might have dire consequences for her at the end of the game.

When she'd started all this, she had told Dugan the truth. She had gone undercover before, but that was just taking on a role in order to be able to get a story. The fact was that she had never been in any actual danger before, not the sort of danger she could be in in this situation. Michael Oren spoke softly, but one look into his eyes told her that there was a cold-blooded man beneath that soft voice.

Maybe she had bitten off more than she could safely chew.

"You're worried, aren't you?" Dugan asked as the day wound down to a close and they were packing up, calling it a day.

Preoccupied, Toni had to replay what he'd just said to her before she could answer him.

"What? No. Why should I be worried?" Toni asked a bit too defensively, bracing herself for another verbal altercation.

She knew exactly what he was saying, Dugan thought, but he went over it anyway. "Because you're starting to realize that Oren isn't the kind of man you can just set up and then go home to your quiet little life."

She didn't like what he was saying. This wasn't a game to her, even if she wasn't on the front lines, dodging bullets. Besides, her life had had its share of turmoil.

"Who says my life is quiet?" she asked him, her back up. "I'm an investigative reporter. There's something going on in my life all the time."

Dugan shrugged. He didn't want to fight with her. Her meeting with Oren was more than a day away. Anything could happen in that time period. She could come to her senses and back out. Or they could wind up catching Oren and taking him out.

"Fine," Dugan told her. "Have it your way."

Turning, he walked away from his desk, leaving her still standing at hers.

"You still want to get that drink?" Toni asked, calling out after him.

Dugan stopped and turned around to look at her. "What drink?" he asked. He was certain he didn't recall saying anything about going out to get something to drink after work today. That had been yesterday's invitation and she had tabled it.

"The one you mentioned getting yesterday," Toni reminded him.

His eyes slid over her. He was right. She *was* nervous. This had to be her way of coping with it, he decided.

"Sure," he answered, beckoning her forward. "I didn't think you were up for it."

"That was yesterday," she told him. "I got some rest last night."

"What about the baby?" he asked. They were almost alone in the squad room right now, but he was in no hurry to leave. She was finally talking to him and it seemed that, for now, her barriers were down.

"She got some rest last night, too," Toni quipped, then smiled. "My nanny doesn't mind staying late with Heather. She's got her own room in my house for the nights she stays over."

"Sound like a pretty good arrangement," Dugan commented.

"Works for me—and for her," Toni told him. She finished gathering her things together. "She likes my house better than her own, anyway."

"No family of her own?" Dugan asked, curious.

She was talking too much, Toni realized. It wasn't her information to share. "What makes you say that?"

The shrug was casual. "Just an assumption. You don't seem to be worried that Lucinda will turn you down if you ask."

He remembered Lucy's name. The guy was a sponge. She was going to have to be careful what she said around him.

"Why do you analyze everything I say?" she asked.

"Sorry," he apologized. She couldn't tell if he was really sorry or not. Was he just trying to get her to let her guard down again? "Occupational habit."

"You're a detective," she pointed out, "not a psychologist."

His smile was rather disarming. "A detective has to be a little bit of everything. Psychologist, priest, mother…"

"Aren't you getting a little carried away here?" she asked with a laugh.

Rather than become defensive, Dugan looked at her very seriously and answered, "Maybe." They had reached the ground floor and headed for the exit. "You want to drive over to Malone's separately, or shall we use my car?"

There wasn't even a moment's hesitation before she answered. "Separately. I'm not staying that long and I want to be able to go straight home without feeling like I'm putting you out for the evening."

He read between the lines and guessed at what was really on her mind. "Don't worry. I won't let you get drunk. Everyone at Malone's kind of keeps an eye out for everyone else," he told her as they walked outside of the building. "We're all cops, so nobody wants to see anyone getting a DUI."

That sounded noble, but she had her doubts about the execution of it. "Isn't it a little hard to tell when a person's had too much to drink?"

"Once in a while, we miss a call," he agreed. "That's when the owners call a cab and have the offending party get driven home."

She would have liked to believe that was true, but she didn't see how it was actually possible. "You make it sound like one big family," she told him, doing her best not to laugh at the idea. In her experience, people who drank were only interested in drinking some more, not in forming a family unit.

Dugan didn't take offense at her skepticism. "Mostly, it is," he told her. "I'd say that at any one time, a third of the cops at Malone's are related to each other. The rest of them belong to the brotherhood—or sisterhood—of cops in general." He smiled at her as they walked into the parking lot. "We watch out for one another. That's what makes it all work."

Pausing by his car, Dugan gave her the address of the bar. "It's about five minutes away. Ten if all the lights are against you," he added. Then, getting into his car, he told her, "See you there," and closed his door.

Toni turned away and got into her own vehicle. Buckling up, she started her car. Dugan's car was right in front of her.

She had second thoughts about going to Malone's and came close to turning around. But because it was June, and thus still light out, she decided it wouldn't hurt for her to spend half an hour unwinding before she went home. Right now, she felt so tightly wound up she could hardly breathe.

In her present condition, she didn't do anyone any good, and while she wasn't the type to turn to alcohol to loosen up, Toni could see the advantage of getting just one drink.

Having to drive home would keep her from going to excess or even having more than that one single serving of beer.

Pulling her car up into a spot behind Malone's, she told herself that she was doing this for background information and that it would add a little balance to her article.

She told herself everything but the truth. That she had gotten herself into something that she wasn't a hundred percent sure she was going to be able to get out of, and maybe unwinding with Dugan was going to help her handle what lay ahead.

The moment she walked into Malone's, Toni instantly felt she had come to the right place. While most of the bars she knew of were dark, somber places where dried-up men nursed beers and looked to pick up willing women, Malone's had an unusually welcoming warmth about it that seemed to just embrace everyone who walked through its doors.

It was also more crowded than she had expected. She scanned the area, looking for Dugan. Several men glanced her way, more than mildly interested.

Maybe it wasn't such a good idea to come here, after all.

"Hey, O'Keefe, over here!" Dugan called out.

A sense of relief washed over her when she heard his voice. She wasn't accustomed to that.

She expected to find him alone. Instead, there were two other men sitting with him as well as a woman. The men both bore a family resemblance. His brothers? she wondered.

Toni thought of making an excuse—that her nanny called, saying there was a problem with the baby seemed reasonable—and just going home. She'd just wanted to grab a quick drink with Dugan. She hadn't counted on meeting other people.

But Dugan headed her off at the pass. Quickly crossing to where she was standing, he took hold of her arm and drew her over to the table where he and the others were already seated.

"On behalf of everyone here," the lone woman at the table said with a quick smile, "I'd like to apologize for Dugan."

"Why?" Toni asked, confused.

"Because he's probably driving you crazy. Dugan believes he knows everything and it's his job to impart that knowledge to the rest of us, because in comparison to him, we're all such slow learners." Rising in her seat, the young woman smiled warmly and stuck out her hand to Toni. "Hi, I'm his cousin, Shayla. That big hulk over there is his brother, Duffy." She pointed out one of the men, then turned toward the other, "And this is our cousin, Finley."

"Finn to my friends," Finley said, rising and putting his hand out right after Duffy had shaken hers. "So, sit down, take a load off," he invited, sitting down himself again.

"That's our Finn, silver-tongued to the very end," Shayla said as she hit his shoulder with the flat of her hand.

"Hey, what did I say?" Finn asked defensively, pretending to rub his shoulder as he looked accusingly at his cousin.

"You don't tell a woman to 'take a load off,'" Duffy said. "Even Dugan here knows that," he said, nodding at his brother.

"Maybe asking you here wasn't such a good idea," Dugan said. "Do you want to leave?"

For the first time since her encounter with Oren and the possible consequences of what she had set up had sunk in, Toni smiled really broadly.

"No, this is nice," she told Dugan, looking around at the others. "Very nice," she emphasized.

"She's being polite," Dugan told the others. "So try to behave like people even though it's against your religion."

"Huh, you should talk," Duffy laughed.

Dugan ignored his younger brother. Turning toward Toni, he asked, "Would you like a beer? Or maybe something stronger?"

"I'll take a light beer," Toni said. "But I can go get my own," she protested when Dugan rose to his feet to get it for her.

"A light beer? Oh, my Lord, that's hardly drinking," Finn commented, rolling his eyes.

"Let the lady have what she wants," Dugan admonished his cousin. He started to walk away, then stopped. "If I leave her here, will she be intact when I come back?" he asked the others.

Finn crossed his heart with his right hand. "We'll be on our best behavior," he promised.

Dugan's skeptical expression remained. He leaned into toward Toni. "Don't believe a word they say," he warned her. "I'll be right back."

"So, we heard about your gutsy move," Duffy told her the moment his brother had walked away and been swallowed up by the crowd.

"My gutsy move?" Toni questioned.

"Telling Oren you'd meet him for dinner. Information gets around," he confided with a wink.

"I'm not doing anything that any one of you wouldn't do," Toni replied, feeling just a little self-conscious about Finn's comment.

"Not true. Finn could have never pulled it off. I know for a fact that he's not Oren's type," Duffy told her.

Shayla leaned forward and put her hand on Toni's, calling her attention to her. "Don't listen to them.

They have no idea how to behave around people. That's why they're going to be bachelors until the day that they both die."

"Hey, I don't see a ring on your finger, Shay," Finn pointed out.

"That's because I'm way too smart to get married," Shayla said with a sniff. "Won't catch me putting up with some guy's garbage day in, day out," Shayla told her cousins.

"Don't think you have to worry in that department," Duffy said with a booming laugh, "Most guys are too smart to come anywhere near you."

"I'm back," Dugan announced, handing the mug of beer to Toni. He looked at the circle of faces, each one more innocent than the other. He knew what that meant. There wasn't an innocent one in the bunch. "We can go sit somewhere else if you'd like," he told Toni.

"No, right here is great," Toni said, her eyes sweeping over the other three at the table. Taking a sip of the beer, she set it down and said, "I was an only child and if I wanted conversation, I had to imagine it. My dad was gone half the time on assignment and he'd leave me to stay with my aunt Janice. She wasn't married and she wasn't much for talking to anyone under the age of twelve."

"Peace and quiet," Shayla said wistfully. Leaning her chin on her upturned hand, she asked, "What was that like? There was always so much noise at the house, I could never even hear myself think."

"You? Thinking?" Duffy questioned with a hoot. "Who are you kidding?"

"You've just encouraged them," Dugan said, sitting down beside Toni. Then he added, "They're not always like this."

"Don't apologize," she told him. "I'm really loving this."

And she was. Listening to his brother and cousins take swipes at one another had her forgetting, for a little while, that she might have done a very dumb thing.

And by the time she got up to leave, half an hour later, her fears had mercifully subsided, at least for the moment. Maybe she'd done the right thing, after all. She would have several police officers strategically scattered throughout the restaurant as well as outside of it and her only job, really, was to draw Oren out and keep him in one place for a little while. The police, she felt confident, would take care of all the rest.

"Sorry about the family," Dugan told her.

He had insisted on walking her outside when she said she had to be going.

"Don't be," she said. "I meant what I said earlier. They were very entertaining. Listening to them, I realized what I'd missed when I was growing up."

Dugan looked at her, as if trying to get at the truth. "Your father really leave you with your aunt all that time?"

Toni nodded. "He did."

"For how long?" Dugan asked. It didn't seem right to him, not when there wasn't a mother in the picture.

"He would be gone a few months at a time. He'd try to take the shorter assignments," she told him. "But then he'd come home and it would be like Christmas. We'd spend time together, doing all sorts of things—until he had to leave again."

He thought of his own parents. "That's not much continuity for a kid."

Toni shrugged. "I didn't know any other way," she confessed. "And it gave me something to look forward to. My aunt wasn't a bad person," Toni told him quickly, defending the woman. "She just didn't know how to relate to a person."

"You mean like those guys in there," he said, meaning his cousins and brother.

"No, she *really* didn't know how to relate. There was a lot of silence in that house," she recalled.

He couldn't really comprehend something like that. Growing up with three brothers, his own house had always been filled with noise. "I can't imagine what that had to be like for you."

"People had it worse," she told him a little defensively.

"I didn't mean to insult you," Dugan said, apologizing.

"You didn't," she said quickly, then relented. "Maybe I'm a bit too sensitive," she admitted. "Well, I'd better get home before Heather puts out a lost poster out on me."

"Sounds very advanced for a two-month-old."

Toni grinned. "She is."

Realizing that she was on the verge of asking him if he wanted to see the baby, she suddenly turned on her heel. Asking him over would be opening up doors she didn't want to open. Yes, he had helped her deliver her baby and there was something about him that she found really attractive—maybe *too* attractive—but she didn't have time for a man in her life right now. She had Heather to think of and take care of. In addition to that, she had a career to continue to nurture. That left absolutely no room for a man in her life, no matter how good-looking and sexy that man might be.

"I've got to go. Bye."

"Bye," he responded. But when he turned around to wave her on her way, Dugan realized that he was talking to himself.

# *Chapter Eleven*

"I'm sorry," Dugan told her. "We're not arguing about this. I'm not about to let you out of my sight and that's final," he said to Toni.

It was the end of the shift, two days later. Somehow, Toni had managed to keep busy and get through the two days between the day she'd set up the dinner with Oren and the actual evening she was to break bread with the cartel kingpin.

The two days had even proven to be rather productive. One of her old contacts had come through and given her the name of someone who was low on the cartel food chain, but who still had access to current information.

Apparently, she told Dugan, according to her contact the next shipment was due into the country in less than a month. The exact location was still a mystery. Which made it more important than ever to be able to capture Oren. He would be their key to finding out the vital information. That, in turn, would allow them to be at the right place at the right time. Without that information, there were just too many drug passageways to stake out and watch over.

"So you're actually planning to shadow me to the restaurant where I'm supposed to meet Oren?" she challenged.

If she was trying to make him feel uncomfortable, Dugan thought, she was failing.

"In a nutshell," he answered, "yes."

"All right," she agreed impatiently. "But that doesn't mean that you need to follow me to my house and wait there while I change."

"Oh, but that's exactly what that means," Dugan told her. "It's faster that way," he said before she could voice a protest.

She voiced it anyway. Angrily. "No, it's not."

She didn't want him coming to her house. That made this all too personal somehow. It was bad enough that she was laying herself bare with Oren. But this taking it a step too far.

"Don't worry," he told her with a grin, "I won't peek. I'll just stay out in the living room, get acquainted."

"With Lucinda?" Toni asked, instantly feeling protective of the younger woman.

He frowned just a little, confused. "I thought you said her name was Heather."

"Wait." She stopped getting her things together and put up a hand. "You're talking about the baby?"

"Yes." Who else would he be talking about? "I thought you understood that."

Toni scowled just a little. He really wasn't making any sense. "You do understand that she's just a little more than two months old and can't tell the difference between you and a bottle of formula."

"Sure she can," he assured her with a laugh. "I don't have any milk."

She pressed her lips together, holding back a cry of frustration. "And why would you even want to meet my baby?"

"Re-meet," Dugan emphasized. "And to answer your question, I helped bring her into the world and I was just curious to see how she was getting along."

She still didn't understand. "Why would you even care?" she challenged, still in the dark.

Dugan spread his hands wide, as if the answer was self-explanatory. "I'm a Cavanaugh, O'Keefe. We like babies."

Toni shook her head as she slipped her purse's shoulder strap onto her shoulder. "You, Dugan Cavanaugh, are a strange, strange man."

He grew just a shade more serious. "That notwithstanding, I don't plan to let you out of my sight tonight until this is all over with," he told her. "Now I'll follow you in my car—and if you're thinking of trying to lose me, don't," he advised, one step ahead of her. "I already know where you live. I had Valri look it up for me."

She was unfamiliar with the name. "Valri?" she asked, waiting for more information.

He nodded. "She's our secret weapon in the computer lab," he told her. They got into the elevator together and his tone changed for a moment when the doors closed. "You don't have to go through with this, you know. You can still change your mind."

She wished he'd stop saying that. Because, even though she wouldn't admit it, it did tempt her. "It's a little late for that, don't you think?"

"No." He looked at her, catching a glimmer of indecision. She *was* having second thoughts, he thought. He talked faster. "I can get one of the detectives to take your place. We've got one who looks enough like you to pass as your twin—almost," he qualified. "We put her in your place, and—"

She had to stop him now, before he got carried away—and took her with him.

"No, I'm not about to back out now," she informed him. "I can handle myself."

"I'm not worried about you handling yourself," he told her honestly.

"Then what's the problem?"

"I'm worried about Oren handling you," Dugan told her.

That made two of them, she thought. But out loud, she said, "That's what I have you for. I get into trouble, you're supposed to come to my rescue, right?"

"That's good on paper," Dugan agreed. "But an awful lot can happen in just the blink of an eye," he pointed out.

"Then I'll be sure not to blink," she answered flippantly.

Dugan made no response. Instead, he merely shook his head. He'd had a feeling that she was a handful the first time he laid eyes on her and he hadn't been wrong—even though he wished differently.

"Let's go," he told her, hustling her toward her vehicle. "I'll be right behind you."

Lucinda's eyes were huge when she opened the front door for Toni and saw the rather tall, handsome detective standing beside her.

"I brought my work home with me, Lucy," Toni told her baby's nanny. Lucinda continued standing where she was, staring.

"I see," Lucinda acknowledged. It took her a full moment to realize that she was blocking the doorway. Coming to, she stepped back, allowing them both to walk into the house. "Hi, I'm Lucy, Heather's nanny," she told Dugan.

It was getting late. She had to get ready, Toni thought. "You don't have to talk to him if you don't want to. He's just here to annoy me."

Lucinda smiled at Dugan. "Can he annoy me?" she asked.

Dugan smiled at the younger woman. It was the kind of smile meant to put her at her ease. "See? Lucy doesn't find me annoying."

"She doesn't know you," Toni answered. "Stay here," she ordered, then added the warning, "And behave. I'll be back in a few minutes."

"So, how did you and Toni meet?" he asked Lucy. "Did she advertise for a nanny, or did you know her before then?"

"Before," Lucinda answered. "I worked in the newspaper office where her father worked. We got friendly. I was his assistant for a while. When I lost that job," she said, breezing over the particulars on purpose, "she, um, took care of me," Lucy concluded.

Dugan did a quick assessment of the young woman and what she had just told him. "I see." She sounded serious, but he wasn't sure if he actually believed her. "And you decided to pay her back by taking care of her daughter while she's at work."

"Yes, yes I did. She was a lifesaver," Lucinda told him. She was about to say something further to him when she stopped, listening. "Sounds like I'm being summoned. If you'll excuse me—"

"Mind if I come along?" he asked, falling into step with her. "I'd really like to see Heather again."

"You've seen her before?" Lucinda asked, caught off guard.

"Just the one time," he answered.

"When?" Lucinda asked, growing suspicious. "I've been around Heather every day and sometimes at night, as well. I don't remember seeing you around."

"Did Toni ever tell you about the night her daughter was born?" Dugan asked as they went up the stairs to the nursery.

"Not really, just that she went into premature labor and—" Lucinda stopped walking again, her eyes widening as she took a closer look at the handsome detective. "*You're* the guy who stopped to deliver Heather?" she asked in complete wonder.

Dugan smiled. "Then she *did* tell you about me."

"Well, she never mentioned you by name," Lucinda told him. "She just said that you came out of nowhere, helped her deliver Heather and then disappeared into the night when your phone rang."

Dugan laughed, nodding. "I guess that covers the essentials." They were on the second floor now, drawing closer to the baby's room. The sound of crying increased two-fold. "I see she still has those lungs," he commented with a smile.

"That she has," Lucinda agreed. "I'm thinking she's going to be an opera singer," she told Dugan as she walked into the nursery. "You've got company, Heather," Lucinda told the baby as she bent over the crib and picked the baby up into her arms.

He was right beside Lucinda. Unlike most babies, who were close to being bald at this tender age, Heather had a full head of hair, and it was dark. He guessed that the baby took after her father, whoever he was.

For just a moment, he wondered what sort of a man had been able to bed Toni, but then he brushed the thought aside. He didn't need to go there. It would only mess things up in his head right now.

"Would you mind if I held her?" Dugan asked.

Lucinda was more than happy to turn the baby over to him for a moment.

"Sure. I don't see why not. But I really hope your

eardrums are strong," she said as she put Heather into his arms.

She expected him to be awkward about the transfer and was really surprised when he took the baby as if he did it all the time. He held her against his chest and looked down at the small face.

Heather's cries abated almost immediately. Quieting down, she looked at him as if she was trying to remember where she had seen his face before.

"Wow, that's amazing," Lucinda marveled, impressed. "She usually doesn't quiet down until I've fed her and changed her. You obviously have a magical touch."

Dugan laughed, patting the baby's bottom. "She just recognizes me, that's all," he said. "Don't you, Heather?" he asked, looking at the baby.

Heather began to make bubbles, still staring up at him as if he had suddenly become the very center of her universe.

"If I didn't know any better, I'd say that you were a baby whisperer," Lucinda told the handsome detective with a laugh.

"I'm just good with kids," Dugan answered, still making eye contact with Heather. "So, how's everything?" he asked the baby. "Any plans for your immediate future? Any flirty boys bothering you that you want me to take care of?"

"She needs her bottle and then she needs to be put to bed," Toni said firmly, coming out of her bedroom. She was surprised to find Dugan up here with Lucinda, but managed to hide that.

"Sounds like a plan to—" Dugan began saying, only to stop dead as he turned around and took a good look at the woman whose body he was going to be guarding tonight. "Wow," he pronounced as he made a full assessment of her. His eyes swept over her again.

Toni saw the appreciation in them and a part of her instinctively preened just a little.

"You clean up really, really nicely, O'Keefe," he told her.

Toni cleared her throat. "I had no idea I was dirty," she quipped. "Did the big bad man scare you, Heather?" she asked, taking her daughter from Dugan and into her own arms.

"Wait, you'd better give her to me," Lucinda said quickly, taking charge. "You don't want her spitting up milk all over your dress, Toni," she cautioned. Heather was apt to do that without warning or provocation for that matter.

Once she had the baby back in her arms, Lucinda turned back to look at Toni. "You look really nice," she said with genuine appreciation. Lucinda smiled. "You two must be going somewhere really special tonight."

Toni suddenly realized what had to be going through the other woman's head. "It's not what you think," Toni told her quickly.

"It's not my place to think anything," Lucinda answered innocently. The next moment, she was unable to hold back a really wide smile that played on her lips. "Just like it's not my place to say that I hope you two have a really nice time together tonight."

The smile on Dugan's face was nonthreatening. "Another time and place, I think we really would," he confided to the young woman. "But tonight isn't that time."

Lucinda looked from Dugan to Toni. It was obvious that she was confused. Still, she didn't seem as if she was about to ask questions.

"Whatever you say," she told Dugan. "But right now, I have a date with a baby and her bottle. Nice to have met you, detective. I hope you and Toni will have fun doing whatever it is you'll be doing."

With that, Lucinda slipped out of the room with the baby.

Toni pressed her lips together and went down the stairs.

"She thinks we're dating," Toni told him.

"I think she's happier thinking that than finding out that I'm actually escorting you into the arms of a drug lord," Dugan answered, telling himself that it was going to be all right tonight.

"You're not escorting me," Toni corrected him. "You're dropping me off in front of the restaurant. Better yet, a block away from the restaurant so that Oren doesn't see you."

Each time he thought about this setup, the worse it sounded to him. "Are you sure that you want to go through with this?"

She stopped at the bottom of the stairs, turning

toward him. "How many times are you going to ask me that?"

"Until I get the right answer, I guess," Dugan answered.

Toni blew out a breath. "I already gave you the right answer. I said yes."

"Oh, before I forget," Dugan said, stopping her before she could get her purse. He dug into his pocket. The next moment, he took out his hand and opened it in front of her. There was a ring in it.

"This is so sudden," Toni quipped putting her hand to her chest.

"Very funny," he commented. "I want you to put this on and keep it on at all times," he told her. "It'll allow us to keep tabs on you."

Although she hadn't seen them, she was aware that there was a whole team of people who were going to be jammed in a van, monitoring her.

Sliding the ring on her third finger, she felt it moving around. "It's a little loose."

"Then put it on another finger," he told her. Rather than wait for her to do it, he took the ring himself and switched it to her index finger. Giving it a tug, he was satisfied. "There, that fits."

Toni held her hand out and looked critically at the ring. It was a delicate aquamarine stone surrounded by a circle of small diamonds. She had to admit that she liked it, but there was no point in saying that to him, or in getting attached to the ring. She'd be giving it back to him once this was over.

"And this is going to pick up everything I say?" she asked him.

"Every breath you take," he answered. Building on that, he told her, "If you start hyperventilating, I'll be there before you can draw another breath." It was a promise.

"Then I'll try to remember not to hyperventilate," she said. She saw the doubtful look on his face and all the fears she'd had earlier—and now—seemed to melt into the background. "Don't worry," she assured Dugan. "I can do this. Just let me get him to start talking a little, make him lower his guard a tad. Who knows, I might be able to get your information for you that way. I can be very persuasive if I want and I can do it without raising his suspicions."

"I sincerely doubt it," he said flatly. "This is a whole different breed of guy. Rules don't apply to him. You just get him comfortable and relaxed and the team and I will do the rest. All right?" he asked, looking at her.

She took a deep breath. "All right," she told him. "Let's do this."

# Chapter Twelve

As Toni walked into the restaurant, she felt as if she was moving in slow motion, trying to use someone else's legs.

The thought really bothered her because she thought of herself as being braver than this. Her slow pace almost made her wonder if age was finally catching up to her—except for the fact that she was only thirty years old and that was way too young to be thinking of herself as getting too old for something.

When had fear suddenly played such a major part in the way she regarded things? Toni upbraided herself. She never used to be like this.

But she realized that her parameters had changed. She didn't just have herself to worry about anymore.

She was responsible for someone else now, a little someone else who had no one but Toni to look after her. Yes, there was Lucinda, but that really wasn't fair of her. Lucy couldn't be expected to look after Heather permanently if something happened to Toni. At twenty-four, Lucinda was hardly more than a child herself in a lot of ways.

If anything, Toni thought, she was actually responsible for two people, not just one. Heather *and* Lucy. That sort of a burden pressed down heavily on her shoulders.

For one thing, it meant that she had to be careful not to take too many chances so that she was able to remain alive.

"May I help you?" the pleasant-faced hostess standing at the hostess table asked.

Preoccupied, Toni quickly collected herself and smiled at the woman. "Yes, I'm supposed to be meeting someone here but I don't see him."

"What's the name of the other party?" the hostess asked her.

"Michael Oren." She was meeting Michael Oren for dinner. Toni couldn't believe she was actually saying that. This was beginning to feel like a B movie from the 1930s, she thought.

The hostess skimmed the list and then smiled. "Oh, yes, I have a reservation for two right here. It's for eight o'clock." She looked up. "He's not here yet, but you're a few minutes early," the hostess pointed out. "Why don't I seat you, and as soon as Mr. Oren comes in, I'll bring him to the table."

Toni nodded. "That would be very nice of you, thank you."

She followed the woman to a table for two that was off to one side. She sat down and the hostess handed her a menu.

"Would you like some wine to drink while you're waiting?" the hostess asked.

"Just water, thank you," Toni responded. Wine always had a way of fogging up her brain and she wanted a clear head. Right now, she needed her A game and that mean steering clear of any alcohol.

"I'll send a busboy," the woman promised as she slipped away.

Almost immediately, a busboy approached her table carrying a pitcher. He poured her a glass of water over ice while she continued looking toward the door.

"Enjoy your water," the busboy told her quietly.

Something in his voice caught her attention and Toni looked up. She realized that she recognized him from the precinct.

Leaning her head on her hand, she whispered, "You have people here." Her lips barely moved.

"What did you expect?" Dugan asked, his voice echoing in her ear via an earwig. "I wasn't about to send you into the lion's den by yourself." And then his voice suddenly changed. "Uh-oh, head's up, O'Keefe. I think your date's here."

Toni looked up, scanning the immediate area. She didn't see Oren.

"Where?" she whispered.

"Just coming in the front door. Showtime, O'Keefe," he told her.

Just then Toni saw Oren walking in through the front entrance.

She felt her hands grow icy cold as she braced herself. This was it. She would have to give the best performance of her life. Toni thought of standing, then decided against it. Instead, she waited until Oren had taken a few steps into the main room. Watching the drug lord, she waited two beats, then raised her hand and waved at him, catching the dapper-looking man's attention.

Seeing the movement, Oren smiled and nodded. His step quickened as he headed toward her table. She saw that there was someone with him. Undoubtedly a bodyguard, Toni thought.

And that was when it happened.

Toni saw the whole thing unfolding almost in slow motion right in front of her eyes. A lone, very solemn-looking dark-haired man had entered the restaurant just behind Oren.

She saw the man put his hand into his jacket.

The next second, in one smooth movement, the man was pulling out a gun. He opened fire.

Oren's bodyguard as well as Oren reacted purely on instinct. As the first bullet whizzed by Oren, he whirled around, simultaneously pulling out his own weapon. His bodyguard had done the same. They started shooting almost at the same time as the other man did.

Complete chaos broke loose.

* * *

Inside the van, Dugan heard the exchange of gunfire. He, as well as several others who were in there with him, immediately bolted out of the vehicle.

"Take cover!" he yelled at Toni even before he made it to the entrance. "Get under a table! Now! Everyone, shots fired! Shots fired!" he cried, alerting the rest of his team.

He was running now, hearing the screams emanating from the restaurant as the people who were trapped inside dove for cover.

Dugan knew his main focus was twofold. He was to catch the shooter and he had to take Oren prisoner. But all he could think of at this moment was that he had to find Toni and somehow get her to safety without any incident.

Running into the restaurant as people came stampeding out, Dugan expected—hoped—to find Toni hiding under a table or seeking shelter somewhere else, out of the line of fire. Instead, he found her only half hidden behind a table that had been pushed down on its side.

She had a gun in her hand.

The same one that he'd seen in her car the night he helped her deliver Heather.

"Damn it, get down out of the way!" he shouted at her across the room as he ran toward her.

Her face was flushed and she was breathing hard. But even now, the chaos was subsiding. Rising from her knees, she was on her feet. "I think I got him," she said. "I hit the shooter in the leg."

At first, it almost sounded as if she was talking to anyone within hearing range, but then it became clear that she was talking to Dugan as she looked over the heads of others toward him.

"The shooter," she repeated. "I think I shot him in the leg."

"Ryan, take your people and fan out. Search the area," Dugan ordered. "The shooter's hurt. He shouldn't have been able to get far. Bring that SOB back to me!"

Several undercover detectives left immediately, searching the entire restaurant as well as the immediate perimeter. However, after more than twenty minutes, they all returned empty-handed. The gunman had gotten away.

Meanwhile, there were several people down, most of them patrons who'd had the misfortunate to be in the way of the shoot-out. At first glance, it didn't look as if there were any casualties. But as Dugan came closer, he saw that Oren and his bodyguard had not only been hit, they were both dead. The gunman had managed to get off more than six shots, of which two had hit the drug lord and one had gotten the bodyguard. Each man had caught a bullet to the head.

Toni came forward, her legs feeling like lead again. There was noise in the background, people talking, but it was all blending into a meaningless roar as she stopped to stand over Oren's body.

Her mouth was so dry, she was having trouble getting the words out. "Is he—is he…?"

"He won't be asking you for a second date,"

Dugan told her quietly. And then he put his hand out for her gun. "I'm going to have to take that from you."

"I have a permit for it," she told him, repeating the same words she had said that first night.

"Still have to collect it. Procedure," Dugan explained. He beckoned over one of his men. "We need ambulances here," he told the man who had brought Toni her water. "At least three of them. Maybe more."

"What about Oren and his bodyguard?" the "busboy" asked, nodding at the fallen drug lord and his henchman.

"The coroner is going to want to see them," Dugan said. "Damn, there goes our chance to question them," he lamented. "Not only that, but now we've got someone from the cartel—or a rival gang—running around out there—or at least hobbling." He didn't like what this meant. Things were escalating. Then, turning toward Toni, he thought of what she'd wound up doing. "Why didn't you tell me you were bringing your gun?"

She said the first thing that came to mind. "You didn't ask."

His expression was grim. "Very funny."

"When can I get that back?" she asked, nodding at the weapon in his hand.

"Later," was all he said. And then he took a closer look at her. Concern was etched on his face. "Are you all right?"

"Fine," she answered. And then her knees buckled. Dugan managed to catch her just before she could hit the floor.

Holding her steady, he eased Toni into a chair. "Here, sit," he told her.

"I'm fine," she repeated. She saw the skeptical look on his face and waved it impatiently away. "I just got a little dizzy, that's all," she mumbled, beginning to get up again.

"I said sit," Dugan ordered, pushing her back down. Pulling another chair over, he sat down next to her. "Take a deep breath." Watching her, he asked, "You want to go to the hospital?"

Toni did what he said. She took a deep breath and blew it out. But she wasn't about to go anywhere. "I don't need to go to a hospital, Cavanaugh. I just need to go home."

"I'm not letting you go anywhere except the hospital in this condition," he told her. "You're shaking."

Toni raised her head defiantly. "No, I'm not."

Ignoring her protest, he stripped off his jacket and draped it over her shoulders. She attempted to shrug it off to give back to him. "I don't need your jacket."

Dugan put it on her shoulders again, his movements a little rougher this time. "Stop arguing with me," he told her. She glared at him but said nothing. "Did you ever shoot at a man before?" he asked, thinking that was why she was shaking this way.

She surprised him by saying, "Once."

"So you're an old hand at this," he said, and Toni couldn't tell if he was mocking her or not.

She looked back at the drug lord's body. Oren was

lying on the floor just a few feet away from her. Had he been closer, she might have wound up on the floor next to him, as dead as he was.

"He's really dead, isn't he? Oren," she specified, nodding over toward the body.

"He's really dead," Dugan confirmed.

She let out another shaky breath. "I just lost you your main source of information."

He looked at her as if she was babbling. "You had nothing to do with it."

"Yes, I did," she insisted. "I saw that guy coming in. I *saw* him draw his weapon. If I had reacted just a little faster, Oren might still be alive."

"Giving yourself a lot of credit, aren't you?" he asked, trying to jar her into reality. "Since when was all this on your head?" he asked. "All you were supposed to do was draw Oren out a little. That was it. Nobody could have predicted this shooter coming in." He turned then to issue orders to his team. "I want all the restaurant surveillance tapes pulled. Somebody get me an ID on that guy," he called out to Winston, one of the detectives.

Winston was on the phone already and he nodded his head in response. "Calling the manager now, boss," he said.

Dugan turned back to Toni. He saw how pale she looked. "Breathe, O'Keefe."

"I *am* breathing," she told him between clenched teeth.

"Breathe deeper," he instructed. "You're in shock

and unless I'm satisfied that you're all right, you *are* going to the hospital."

"I'm breathing, I'm breathing," she told him grudgingly.

"Conway, watch her," Dugan said as he got up. His intent was to go talk to some of the witnesses. He wanted to get their names down as well as their cursory summaries of what had happened from their points of view.

But before he could take a single step away from her, Toni was on her feet.

"I am not an invalid and I'm not a prisoner. I don't need to be *watched*," she said. "What I am is a trained investigative journalist who knows how to ask questions. I can help you," she insisted, in no uncertain terms. Then, softening, she made it a request. "Let me help. Please."

He wanted to tell her to go sit down. To just stay out of his way and be glad that she was alive. Heaven knew that he was.

The words hovered on the tip of his tongue as he looked at her face. But he could see that she needed to be doing something so that she wouldn't dwell on what had just happened and what had *almost* happened to her. He could understand that.

He'd been there himself a time or two, Dugan recalled. He really didn't want to, but he relented.

"All right," Dugan said grudgingly. "But if I let you come with me, you have to promise me that you're not going to get in the way." Toni was already nodding her head, but he stopped her before she could say anything. "That means no talking unless I specifically ask you a question. Understand?"

She took a breath and nodded. "I understand."

Her expression told him that she didn't like it, but that she was willing to go along with what he was proposing. Anything was better than being a bump on a log in her estimation.

"No talking," she repeated.

He highly doubted that she would stick to her word, but at least he had laid down the ground rules. That meant that if she didn't listen, he would be able to send her home if he wanted to.

The next several hours were painful. The restaurant patrons and the staff were really shaken up, and it was a while before Dugan and his people were able to gather all the information that they needed.

He discovered, much to his amazement, that despite being shaken up herself, rather than being a liability, Toni turned out to be a huge asset when it came to calming people down. As a civilian, rather than a police detective or officer, she was able to relate to the people on a level that he and his team couldn't.

Moreover, she picked up on small things, asked them questions about their families and, also as a civilian, she could relate to their trauma.

She was able to get one woman to stop sobbing and finally talk to them, describing what she had seen. Hers had been the first table the shooter had passed before he opened fire. Her description turned out to be extremely useful.

Slowly but surely, statements were collected and people were either taken to the hospital or released and allowed to go home.

Finally, every one of the patrons had cleared out, leaving only the manager and a skeleton crew in their wake. They were preparing to leave, as well.

"Hell of a cleanup tomorrow morning," the manager lamented, shaking his head as he surveyed the chaos that was left.

"I'm afraid not," Dugan told the man.

The manager looked at him in irritated disbelief. "Why not?"

"Our crime scene investigators are going to need to go over everything before you can start the cleanup."

"They're not finished yet?" The manager glared at the three men who were gathering what appeared to him to be little more than tiny scraps.

"I'm afraid not. Not by a long shot," Dugan said, attempting to be comforting.

"How long are they going to be?" the man demanded, clearly upset.

"Hard to say," Dugan answered honestly. "All I can tell you is that we'll be as quick as possible," he promised.

It was a promise that the frazzled manager obviously didn't believe and didn't find comforting in the slightest.

"Yeah, yeah," he complained. "I should have become an engineer like my mother wanted me to," he said under his breath as he walked out of the restaurant. The door slammed behind him.

"Okay," Dugan said, turning to Toni. "Time to go." Once they began to walk out, he said, "I owe you an apology."

She wasn't sure just what to make of what he was saying.

"For what?" Toni asked cautiously.

"You turned out to be a tremendous asset tonight," he admitted. "I don't think I would have been able to calm that one woman down if it hadn't been for you."

Toni shrugged. "I'm good with hysterical people," she told him. "Once I stop being hysterical myself," she added with a self-deprecating smile.

They were outside the restaurant now and he recalled that she still hadn't had anything to eat. "Why don't I take you somewhere? You never got a chance to have dinner."

It was almost eleven o'clock. She pressed her hand against her abdomen.

"Not sure I could face food."

"Coffee, then," he suggested. "And then I'm driving you home."

He seemed to have forgotten one important point. "But my car—" she began to protest.

"Don't worry about it. I'll have an officer drive it home for you."

"Then how will he be able to get back?" she asked.

He could only shake his head in wonder. After

what she'd been through, she was still able to worry about someone else.

"The officer following him will drive him back. Any other questions?"

Toni shook her head. "No. But if I think of any, I'll ask."

He laughed to himself as he escorted her to his car. "Yes, I'm sure you will."

# *Chapter Thirteen*

"Don't you have to go to the precinct, fill out some kind of report about what just happened?" she asked Dugan as they sat in a booth in a small, all-night restaurant. Except for one other couple, they were the only ones there.

"I've got other people working on that," Dugan told her.

Ordinarily, he didn't delegate things. He would have been at the precinct right now, filing a report about how the case had gone down. But he'd opted to use his judgment, and right now he felt he could do more good here, sitting with her, than anything he could wind up accomplishing at the precinct. Oren and his bodyguard were dead, just like his CI was, another murder he had yet to solve.

Moreover, the shooter was currently in the wind, but there were half a dozen police officers still out looking for him. He doubted that they would find the man, but there was always hope.

He nodded at the coffee cup Toni was holding. "Sure I can't get you anything?"

"You didn't even have to get me this," she pointed out. And then she smiled ruefully. He'd gone out of his way to be nice to her and she was being blasé about it. She knew why she was behaving this way. Because she was attracted to him and she was trying to keep him at a distance so she wouldn't give herself away. "I'm sorry. I have trouble saying thank-you sometimes."

"Really?" he asked, feigning surprise. "I hadn't noticed." And then the smile on Dugan's face vanished and he grew serious. He was worried about her. He tried to tell himself that his reaction was just routine—but it wasn't and he knew it. "You don't have anything to thank me for. If anything, I should be apologizing. I put you in harm's way."

"No," she argued, "*I* put me in harm's way, remember? Whatever happened tonight, *I* was the one who got the ball rolling. If I hadn't pretended to trip and fall into Oren's arms, none of this would have happened." She sighed, shaking her head. "I honestly thought I was doing some good, getting the ball rolling for you."

He studied her for a long moment. She began to grow uncomfortable before he finally asked, "You always do this?"

"Do what?" she asked, unclear as to what he was talking about.

"Beat yourself up like this," Dugan answered. "Because it's pointless. Just stop," he told her. "You could examine this from a thousand different angles, but that's not going to change anything that happened. Nobody can successfully predict the future. You tried to help, but there was no way for you to know that your plans were going to be blown to smithereens by a shooter from a rival cartel."

"Is that what he was?" Toni asked, suddenly coming to life. "He was from a rival gang?"

"The lab went over the footage from the surveillance cameras and managed to get a hit pretty quick. The shooter was David Padilla. His people belong to the Sinaloa Cartel and they've been trying to cut the Juarez Cartel out of the drug business in Mexico for the last eighteen months. I guess they just decided to bring their turf war here."

"I shot someone from a rival drug cartel?" Toni asked, trying to wrap her mind around the import of that information.

"That you did." Trying to lighten the mood, he grinned as he put his cup of coffee down. "Maybe I should start calling you Annie Oakley."

She hardly heard him. Instead, she was thinking about what he had just said about the other man. "If you know who he is, can't you go and arrest him?"

"Go where?" he asked. "It's not like I can just wander up to the local drug-lords-are-us and round the guy up."

"What *can* you do?" Toni asked. As far as she was concerned, this was unfinished business. There was someone out there who could have very well killed her while he was shooting at Oren. The thought of it made her feel nervous.

Dugan said to her what he would have said to anyone in this situation—and hoped it would satisfy her. "We wait until we hear word about another shipment that's coming in, or we get information that allows us to conduct a local drug bust and get someone to flip on Padilla in exchange for a lesser sentence."

She read between the lines. "But that's not anytime soon, is it?"

"You never know," he told her evasively.

She frowned. What he was saying was hardly a course of action. There had to be something else. Something *she* could do.

"I can try putting the word out," Toni finally said to him.

"You?" Dugan questioned. What sort of "word" was she talking about?

She could see that he didn't believe her. But she did have credentials in this game. She just hadn't been specific before because she couldn't be. "I know people who know people."

That sounded incredibly vague but he had an idea that she wasn't just talking. His face clouded up. "Listen to me. I do not want you getting any more mixed up in this than you already are."

If she closed her eyes, she could see it all happening again. The shooter, the people screaming. Oren dropping practically at her feet. His bodyguard going down at the same time. "I think it's too late for that."

Dugan tried to appeal to her as a mother. "Don't you want to stay home for a bit, watch that beautiful little girl of yours grow?"

He had inadvertently hit on the wrong strategy. This whole thing was about Heather, as well as Lucinda before her. "What I want is for that beautiful little girl to be proud of her mother."

"And she can't be proud of you unless you're instrumental in bringing down a drug cartel?" he asked sarcastically.

Toni merely smiled at him as she finished the last of her coffee.

Dugan shook his head. "You are really in a class all by yourself, O'Keefe."

Toni inclined her head. "I'll take that as a compliment."

"I'm not sure if I intended it to be one," he told her honestly.

He took a breath. There was no point in pursuing this matter. He had a feeling that she could probably argue this thing right into the ground without a resolution.

Dugan changed the subject. "Say, it's almost Saturday," he said out of the blue. "What are you doing this weekend?"

He'd caught her totally off guard. "Why?" she asked suspiciously.

"I've got this family get-together to go to and I thought maybe you'd like to come along." The more he thought about it, the more convinced he was that this was the right way to go with her. "Might do you some good."

She almost asked "why" again, but the import of his unspoken intent suddenly hit her. "Are you asking me out, Cavanaugh?"

"More like 'in' actually," Dugan corrected. "I'm asking you in to a family gathering."

"What's the occasion?" If this was a gathering, it had to be for a reason.

He shrugged. "No occasion," he answered. Andrew had decided he felt like having the family over and that was enough for everyone else.

No occasion. That didn't make any sense to her. "There has to be an occasion," Toni insisted.

Dugan laughed. "Not with my family there doesn't." And then, because he could see that didn't satisfy her, he gave her a little background. "My uncle Andrew used to be the chief of police here in Aurora. He misses the charged energy that entailed," he told her. "Having a house full of cops makes him feel like he's still in the game, so to speak."

Toni pressed her lips together, shaking her head. "Well, I don't understand any of it, but sure, why not?" She felt it would give her another layer to add to the article when she finally wrote it. "You sure he won't mind my coming along?"

"Mind?" Dugan laughed again. "Hell, he's the first one who always says the more the merrier." Which made Dugan think of something else. "As a matter of fact, why don't you bring Heather?"

She stared at him. "You're pulling my leg."

The smile that curved his mouth was nothing short of sexy and hot. Tired though she was, Toni felt herself growing decidedly warmer.

"Not that that might not be an interesting endeavor," Dugan said, "but no, I'm not. Kids are invited, too. Uncle Andrew likes having family around."

"You forgot one little thing—I'm not family," she pointed out.

Strictly speaking, she was right. But there was nothing about Andrew that made the man slavishly adhere to any rules.

"No," he agreed, "but you're the next best thing. You're a lady with a baby."

"You really are serious," she realized in surprise.

"Completely," he answered simply.

"Okay, you're on," Toni said gamely. And then she looked at her watch. "But right now, I need to be getting home. It's getting really late and poor Lucy's been taking care of Heather for a really long time today."

She knew that there were no hard-and-fast rules when it came to the amount of time that Lucy put in, but she felt this was taking advantage of the young woman.

"How much work can a two-month-old baby be?" Dugan asked, amused.

Toni could only shake her head. "Spoken like a man with no children," she told him. And then she remembered something. "Oh, are you sure that someone will drive my car to my house?"

"Already done," he assured her. "I gave Braden your address when I left with you," he said, mentioning another officer.

Her head felt as if it was spinning. "You do think of everything, don't you?" she marveled.

"I try," he answered. "You ready to go?"

Rather than answer him, she slid out of the booth and stood up.

"Okay, I guess you are," he acknowledged. "After you," he said, gesturing for her to lead the way.


"You really don't have to bring me right up to my door you know," she told him. "I'm perfectly capable of reaching it by myself."

His smile was easy. "My mother taught me to always make sure a woman got home safely."

"I'm sure she meant that about your dates, not women you're working a case with," she pointed out.

The moment she said them, the words sounded rather lofty to her. She really wasn't working this case with him, she was being swept up in the ensuing tide. But that didn't change the fact that she really *wanted* to be of help.

"My mother didn't really differentiate," was all he said. They were at her door now. "I'll be by to pick you and Heather up tomorrow around noon. Is that all right with you?"

"Sure, noon's fine," she told him. "I'll see you then."

Toni put her key in the lock, then hit a combination of numbers to disarm the security system. Turning to look over her shoulder, she saw that Dugan was still exactly where she'd last seen him. She'd just assumed that he would have backed away by now and gone to his vehicle.

"You're still here," she said.

"Just waiting for you to go inside and rearm your security system," he told her simply.

"Are you always this thorough?" she asked.

His smile was wide and beguiling. "As a matter of fact," he told her, "Thorough happens to be my middle name."

She merely shook her head. That wouldn't have been the name she would have gone for. "Persistent" was more like it.

"If you say so." Opening the door, Toni crossed the threshold and then closed the door behind her. She hit the numbers on the keypad located by the doorjamb. Because she knew he was still standing there, she asked, "Satisfied?"

"Is it armed?" Dugan asked, his voice coming through the door.

He heard her sigh. "Yes, Cavanaugh, it's armed."

"Then, yes, I'm satisfied," he told her. "Good night, O'Keefe."

He heard her laughing on the other side of the door. "Good night, Cavanaugh."

Dugan had parked his car at the curb right in front of her house. He walked to it now. Getting in, he started it up, then pulled away.

Knowing that she was watching him, he waved once as he drove off.

"Good night, Cavanaugh," she repeated to herself before she let the curtain on the living room window drop back into place.

Kicking off her shoes, she went up the stairs.

"That police detective didn't spend the night here, did he?" Lucinda asked her the following morning as she walked into the kitchen.

Because it had been late by the time Toni came home, Lucy had decided to spend the night rather than drive to her place. She was seriously considering Toni's offer to give up her apartment and just live at her house. It would certainly save her some money, and she did like Toni's house better than her own place.

But she didn't want to get in the way, and if Toni was entertaining the police detective, that might complicate matters.

"No, he did not," Toni informed her. She saw the expression on Lucy's face and decided to be honest with her. "Not that I wasn't tempted to invite him in after yesterday—"

"Why? What happened yesterday?" Lucinda asked eagerly.

Toni realized her mistake. She didn't want Lucy being worried, especially not needlessly. So she waved her own words away.

"It's too complicated to get into before my morning coffee," Toni told her. "Maybe even too complicated to get into *after* my morning coffee," she added with a self-deprecating laugh.

It wasn't that she hid things from Lucinda, but she didn't want to worry the other woman, either. She wasn't certain just how Lucy would take the news about the shoot-out that she'd found herself in the middle of last night. Toni decided that she needed to put time and distance between herself and the incident before she could honestly talk about it.

"Why would you ask me that, anyway?" Toni asked.

Having gotten herself a large mug of coffee, she sat down with it and took her first long, bracing sip, letting the hot liquid wind almost seductively through her system.

"Because I think that's his car outside," Lucinda answered.

About to take another sip, Toni stopped with the mug just halfway to her lips. Her eyebrows drew together.

"What? No. That's impossible. I saw him drive away last night," Toni told Lucy. "You've made a mistake."

Lucinda shrugged, letting the living room curtain drop.

"Guess that's just another car that looks like his. But the funny thing is, it's been parked across the street most of the night."

Putting the mug down on the table, Toni crossed over to the living room to look out the window. "How would you know that?"

"I got up at two to make sure that the security system was armed—I thought that maybe you forgot to do it," Lucinda explained.

"Once," Toni told her, holding up her index finger. "I forgot to arm it once."

Lucy flushed. "I know, but I just wanted to be sure. You did, by the way," she added. "Arm it, I mean," she explained. "But I saw that car parked across the street and I thought it was rather odd. Anyway, the car's still parked there, so I wondered if maybe you and the detective had, you know…"

"No, the detective and I didn't 'you know,'" Toni told her. She took another, longer look at the car that was parked across the street.

"What are you going to do?" Lucinda asked her. She glanced at the one landline in the house that Toni kept in case the cell phones went down. "You want me to call the police?"

She had to admit that calling the police was the first thought that crossed her mind, as well, mainly because of the previous night's shooting and the rival cartel gunman who had managed to escape. Her bullet had been in his leg. For all she knew, it still might be, but even if it wasn't, she was certain that he was the type of man who would want revenge for that.

All sorts of thoughts were crowding into her head, such as that somehow the shooter had managed to follow her home and was staking out her place, waiting for her to emerge.

Toni paused, taking a breath. She was getting carried away. In all likelihood, the car parked across from her house belonged to someone else in the area—or maybe it belonged to someone who was entertaining an overnight guest.

There were a hundred and one possible reasons that particular car had been there all night. However, that didn't help calm her down.

"Is something wrong?" Lucinda was asking her. "You look like you've just gotten a little paler than before."

"It's the lighting," Toni answered quickly. "These lightbulbs always make me look like I'm washed out." She thought a moment and then made up her mind. "Lucy, I'm going to check out that car. Close the door behind me when I leave. If you see anything go wrong, *anything at all*," Toni stressed, although still trying not to alarm the other young woman, "I want you to call 911 immediately."

Lucy looked at her, growing nervous and distressed. "Wait, what do you mean, 'go wrong?' Toni, are you sure you don't want me to call the police? Who's in the car?" she asked.

"I'm not sure," Toni answered truthfully. "Probably nobody." Toni paused, looking out the window again. She could make out someone in the car, but not who it was. "Just do as I say, all right?"

"Why don't you stay in the house?" Lucinda asked, catching hold of her arm. "We'll call the police together."

"I never liked being a sitting duck," Toni told her. "Just do as I say, all right?" she repeated.

The next moment, she went outside, closing the door behind her.

## Chapter Fourteen

By the time Toni was halfway across the street, she could make out the features of the person who was sitting in the driver's seat. It was Dugan. He appeared to be dozing.

Why was he out here?

Walking up to the car, she knocked on the window, managing to startle him.

Dugan's hand was instantly on the butt of his weapon before he realized it was her. Taking his hand off his gun, he turned the engine key in order to roll down his window.

"What are you doing here?" Toni asked the second he could hear her.

Dugan rotated his shoulders, doing his best to get out the kink between his shoulder blades.

"Sleeping, apparently," he answered ruefully.

Dugan couldn't remember when he'd fallen asleep. The last thing he remembered was that it was a little after three thirty. The activity on the street had been nonexistent for hours by that time.

"What *were* you *supposed* to be doing here?" she asked, rephrasing her question. The last she knew, he was driving home. He had to have doubled back. "Have you been here all night?"

He answered her questions in the order received. "Guarding you and yes."

"Guarding me?" Toni echoed, her eyes widening as she looked at him. "Why?" she asked. "Am I in some kind of danger? What have you heard?"

She looked back at the house, concerned. It was one thing to put herself in danger, but quite another to involve Lucinda. Maybe she should send the young woman home right now.

"No, you're not in any danger," he told her quickly. "I'm just being overly cautious—and apparently not doing too good a job at it." He could see he wasn't convincing her. "If you were actually in danger, I wouldn't have fallen asleep," he said. "I'm a better detective than that."

Toni pressed her lips together, thinking. She could spot most people lying a mile away, but Dugan was another matter.

Giving up for the moment, she asked him, "You want to come in for some coffee—and breakfast?"

The detective didn't answer her immediately.

Instead, he had an expression on his face that she couldn't quite read.

Instantly on edge, she asked him, "What's the matter?"

That was when she saw the glimmer in his eyes. "I'm trying to decide whether to be noble and turn you down, or be honest and say yes."

"Honest is always better," Toni assured him firmly.

"Then yes," Dugan told her, opening his door and getting out. "I'd love to come in for coffee and breakfast." He judged that he had a little time to spare, but not all that much.

"You know the way, detective," Toni told him, turning around and walking back to her front door.

When he followed her into the living room, he found that Toni wasn't alone. Lucinda was standing in the doorway leading to the kitchen, holding the baby in her arms.

"Welcome back, detective," she told him cheerfully. "Are you staking us out?"

"Just keeping the peace," he replied, smiling at her. "Where's your bathroom?" he asked, turning toward Toni. "I'd like to splash some water in my face, try to look human."

"You look pretty human to me," Lucinda murmured, returning his smile.

"Thank you," Dugan said, then looked toward Toni, waiting.

Toni pointed to the far left of the house. "There's

one down here, right off the family room before the garage door," she told him.

"Be right back," Dugan replied.

Lucinda waited until the detective had disappeared around the corner before turning back toward Toni. There was a big grin on her face.

"The detective seems pretty interested in you," she commented.

Caught off guard, Toni mumbled something unintelligible under her breath, then said, "Lucy, you've been watching too many romantic comedies. Detective Cavanaugh is in the middle of an investigation, and if he's interested in anything at all, it's in finally bringing down a major drug dealer, not me." Even as she said the words, Toni rolled her eyes.

But Lucinda merely smiled. "If you say so. Let me just change Heather and I'll make breakfast," the younger woman offered.

"That's all right. Just change the baby's diaper. I'll take care of breakfast," Toni said, heading into the kitchen and grabbing an apron.

Lucinda stood in the doorway, about to leave. "That's right. I forgot. You can cook."

"Very funny," Toni answered. Opening the refrigerator, she took out six eggs as well as a loaf of bread and placed them on the counter.

"What's very funny?" Dugan asked as he came into the kitchen.

"Nothing," Toni told him. Then, because he continued looking at her as she poured a cup of coffee for him, she said, "You wouldn't understand. It's a private joke."

Approaching him, she grew serious as she lowered her voice. "Tell me the truth, are we in any danger?" she asked, shifting the subject back to him and why he had spent the night in his car, watching over her.

"I am being honest," he answered. "It's just me, being overly protective. But if you're worried," he added, "I can post a police officer in a squad car to keep watch for a few days."

Toni shook her head. "No. I guess that I'm the one being paranoid. Padilla doesn't know who shot him and he certainly doesn't know where I live. Besides," she went on, "I've been threatened before and it never turned out to be anything."

Dugan sat down at the table. "The gun in your car," he recalled. "You never did tell me about that." His implication was clear. He wanted to hear about the incident now.

She was about to reiterate that it was nothing, but she saw that he wasn't going to let it go at that. So she told him. "Just some guy who claimed I ruined his business and his life."

"That doesn't sound like nothing," Dugan answered.

"I wrote an exposé on this man's dealings. I didn't fully appreciate it at the time, but he was involved in what turned out to be a mini pyramid scheme." Her expression darkened as she recalled the details. "The guy was taking people's life savings and 'investing' them. Turns out what he was doing was just lining his own pockets. He must have stolen money from a hundred people like that, maybe more.

"He eluded the police for a while. I kept posting updates on him, using anything I could find. That was when he started threatening me." She shrugged. "They have him now and he's awaiting trial." She smiled at him. "It's all good."

Dugan wasn't entirely satisfied with her answer or with her blasé attitude. He made a mental note to look up the case she was talking about. "What's this guy's name again?"

"He had a lot of aliases, but it boiled down to Jimmy Philbrooks." She took a breath. "So, scrambled or sunny-side up?" she asked him.

"Surprise me," Dugan answered, then he looked at his watch and added, "Just as long as it's fast, I'm not really fussy."

She broke the eggs into a giant pan. "You're in a hurry?"

"You might say that," he told her. "I've got to get down to the precinct to check something out, then swing by my place to change before I come back here to pick you and Heather up."

"Are we still doing that?" she asked as the toast popped up in the toaster. Taking all three slices out, she buttered the bread quickly, placing each on a separate plate.

"Absolutely," Dugan answered. And then he looked at her. "Unless you've changed your mind and don't want to go."

"No, I'd love to go," she assured him. "I just thought that with all you've got going on today, you might want to pass on your uncle's gathering."

Dugan grinned, doing justice to the plate she'd just placed before him. "Unless I'm dead—or giving birth—neither of which will probably be the case, I'm expected to show up, at least for part of the day. So, no, I'm not passing on it."

"What if you're sick?" she asked as she got Lucinda's plate ready.

"We Cavanaughs are an amazingly healthy breed. To my best recollection, I don't remember anyone ever getting sick." And then he told her the added incentive. "Uncle Andrew's an amazing cook."

"You mean, for a police chief," she said, assuming that was what Dugan meant by his compliment.

"No, for anyone," Dugan told her. "I think that most of us, even if we did get sick, would crawl on our hands and knees to make sure that we got our share. Really," he added when he saw the skeptical expression on her face. Then he shrugged with a smile. If he said too much, it might have the opposite effect. "You can judge for yourself," he told her. "Not that this isn't good," he added quickly, concerned that Toni might think that he was belittling her efforts in some way.

Toni laughed, putting her own breakfast onto a plate now. "Don't worry. I don't take offense over anything—except for criticism of my writing."

"I'll keep that in mind," he told her. Finished, he retired his fork.

"You wolfed that right down," Toni marveled. "Did you even taste it before you swallowed it?"

"I did and it was very good," he told her, standing up. "But if I'm going to be back in time to take you to Uncle Andrew's, I've got to leave now." *And if I don't leave right now, I might wind up doing something stupid and scare you off.* He was feeling a very strong pull toward this woman. He told himself to keep his guard up.

Picking up the plate, he took it over to the sink and put it in, much to Toni's surprise. "I'll see you in a few hours. Tell Lucinda goodbye for me," he added.

Toni walked him to the door. "If you find that you can't come back later, that's all right. I'll understand," she assured him.

Dugan stopped for a minute, taking a long look at her face. She'd really been hurt before. He found himself hating a man he didn't know. "You really expect me to bail on you, don't you?" he asked.

"Let's just say I've learned not to count on anything too much," Toni answered. "Disappointment is the name of the game," she said cavalierly.

"Noon," he told her. He pointed to the keypad by the inside of the door just before he left. "And don't forget to rearm the system."

"I don't need to be reminded," she answered through the door as she keyed in the code.

"I know. I just like saying it," he told her, his voice fading as he hurried back to his vehicle and got in.

Shaking her head, Toni went back to the kitchen and her cooling scrambled eggs.

* * *

"I still can't believe you came back," she said.

It was four hours later and they were on their way to the former chief of police's house. He had even remembered to put the baby's car seat into the back without any prompting to insure that Heather would be safe.

Toni had just assumed that if Dugan did come back for her, he would have changed his mind about taking along the baby. After all, babies required a lot of supplies of their own everywhere they went. It was just a given. And he was a bachelor, which meant that his mind didn't operate on that level.

Or so she had thought.

But she had obviously thought wrong.

"I said I would," he reminded her. "And if nothing else, I'm a man of my word."

"Apparently," Toni agreed. Turning in her seat, she looked back doubtfully at the baby. Heather was dozing now, but that could change at any moment. "Are you certain that your uncle won't mind us just dropping in on him like this?"

"I told you, it's an open invitation," he told her. "And I doubt if there's a man around who is friendlier than Uncle Andrew, although a couple of my other uncles run a close second," he had to admit.

It sounded like an ideal family. Definitely the kind of family she would have loved to have had. She dearly loved her father, but she hadn't gotten to see him all that much, given the nature of his work. And then, finally, when he did have some time to spend with her, he'd died.

Still, she couldn't just insert herself into someone else's family, even though it sounded tempting. It didn't seem right.

"But the invitation, as I understand it, is for police personnel, right?" she asked, trying to make her point.

He glanced at her for a second, then looked back to the road. "It's not an exclusive invitation, if that's what you mean."

Toni shook her head. "I'm a journalist," she argued. "Don't most cops *hate* journalists?"

In her experience, they thought of journalists as invaders. She didn't want to stick out like a sore thumb at this gathering.

"Do you lie for a living?" he asked her suddenly.

Stunned, she looked at him. Where had that come from? "No," she cried, taking offense.

"Calm down," he laughed. "What I'm trying to say is that as long as you tell the truth, Uncle Andrew will love you. He really values the truth," Dugan assured her. "The truth and babies," he added with a grin, glancing up into the rearview mirror to look at the sleeping baby. "It's been a while since we've had a newborn around the place," he told her.

"Heather's closing in on almost two and a half months," she pointed out.

He laughed, disregarding her protest. "Oh, but she still has that new baby smell."

Toni's eyes crinkled as she looked back at her sleeping daughter. "I guess she does, at that."

"You know, Lucinda could have come along, too," Dugan told her.

"And both of us appreciate the invitation," she told him. "But Lucy could really use some time off. She hasn't been away from Heather for the last week. Much as she loves my daughter, I know that she'd like some time to herself. Having some free time is really nice, too."

Toni looked out the window and was amazed to see that there were many cars of all sizes parked up and down the block on both sides as well as several blocks beyond that.

"Wait." She did a double take. "All these cars belong to people in your family?"

He thought he'd explained all this and that she knew what she was getting herself into.

Maybe not, he decided.

"Well, I can't vouch for every one of these vehicles, but yes, in all likelihood, these all belong to someone in the family."

"All right, here's a question for you. Just exactly where are you going to park?"

He waved off the question. "There's always someplace. If not here, then around the development's green space. Tell you what," he suggested. "I can let you off right here with the baby. Just go on up to the house. The door's most likely not locked. Meanwhile, I'll go look for parking."

She was *not* about to walk into someone's house,

especially not one that belonged to the former chief of police. The man didn't know her, and neither did most of his family.

"No, that's all right. I'd rather wait and come in with you," she told him.

"Okay, but just remember, I offered," Dugan said to her.

As it turned out, Dugan got lucky. A neighbor had just pulled out across the street, leaving a space by the curb. The space was for a compact car. His Mustang fit that description to a T.

He quickly zipped into the space.

The second Dugan turned off the engine, Heather woke up. With the comforting rocking motion at an end, the baby began to whimper and very quickly to cry in earnest.

Toni frowned. This was exactly what she hadn't wanted.

"This is not a good way to make an entrance," she commented.

Dugan got out of the vehicle, locking it.

"Don't worry about it. Here, give her to me," he told her.

Before she could offer a protest, Dugan took the baby from her. He tucked his arms around the small, noisy bundle.

Heather's cries subsided into a whimper. As she gazed up at him with her electric blue eyes, the whimper ceased altogether. She looked as if she was completely fascinated by what she saw.

Toni could only stare at him in utter amazement. "How do you *do* that?"

"I guess it's just my natural charm," Dugan replied with only a hint of a smile. He made a small face at the baby, then looking at Toni, he said, "C'mon, let's show her off to the family."

She didn't want to say anything in reference to his comment, but for just the smallest of moments, Toni had to admit that what he'd just said to her had a really good sound to it.

"Lead the way," she told him, picking up the diaper bag and the large shoulder bag that she had taken to carrying with her on the rare field trips that she undertook with Heather.

But Dugan would have none of it. "Here," he told her. "Give me that."

Before she could argue with him, he had taken the large diaper bag from her and, still carrying Heather in his arms, he went up to the front door.

# Chapter Fifteen

Andrew Cavanaugh was a tall, striking man who looked a great deal younger than his actual sixty years. Still in trim fighting form, his thick head of hair was just beginning to turn gray but his face was completely without the telltale lines of a hard life, despite the things he had endured.

He was in the foyer, on his way to the kitchen, when Dugan walked in carrying Heather. Toni was right behind him.

Andrew stopped and smiled broadly at them and at the baby. "Recruiting them a little young, aren't we?" he asked Dugan.

"Never too early to start," Dugan quipped. "Uncle Andrew, this is Toni O'Keefe's daughter, Heather."

"Pleased to meet you, Heather." Andrew raised his

eyes to look at the young woman beside his nephew. "And I take it that you're Toni O'Keefe?"

Toni put her hand out to shake his. "Yes, sir."

Andrew shook her hand. "I knew a Tony O'Keefe. But he certainly didn't look anything like you," the chief told her with a warm, welcoming smile.

Toni smiled, feeling an instant kinship. "Tony was my father. You knew my father?" she asked, pleased and surprised.

Andrew nodded. "He was a hell of a newspaper-man in his day. Always knew you were getting a square deal with him. How's he doing?" Andrew asked. "Do you mind?" He indicated the baby.

"Go right ahead," Toni told him, stepping back. "Dad died a few years ago," she said, answering Andrew's other question.

"I'm sorry to hear that. There weren't many journalists like him. He'd go after a story no matter where it took him, and he didn't stop until he had it. But you never felt that he was sacrificing people for the story." Taking the baby into his arms, he looked at Toni. "You're a journalist, too, aren't you?"

Toni nodded. "I thought I'd follow in his foot-steps."

Andrew looked at her more closely. Recognition entered his eyes. "You're the one who was in that shootout at the restaurant yesterday."

Toni glanced at Dugan. "You're right, he does know everything."

Andrew laughed. "I just like keeping my finger in the pie, knowing what my family is up to. Well,

I'd better get back to the kitchen and get busy before I start having to field complaints from everyone that dinner's late." He transferred the baby back to Dugan. "It's really nice meeting you, Toni. I hope you enjoy yourself today. Oh—" He stopped for a moment, looking back at her. "If you want to put your daughter down for a nap later, have Lila show you to the nursery," he told her, mentioning his wife. "You'll find a couple of cribs in there."

Toni looked at Dugan quizzically the moment that the chief walked away. "Nursery? Cribs? Isn't he a little old to have those in his house?"

"The chief brought the cribs down from the attic when the next generation of Cavanaughs started making their appearance." Dugan smiled down at the baby in his arms. "They never stopped." Glancing toward Toni, he told her, "Uncle Andrew is nothing if not prepared."

But Toni was focused on something else at the moment. "You didn't tell me that he knew my father."

"I didn't know," Dugan answered. "But to be honest, it doesn't really surprise me. Uncle Andrew seems to know everyone, or did at one point or another. All right," he said, changing subjects. "Let's get you introduced around to the troops."

The first person whose path they crossed was someone Toni already knew.

"Hey, I like your accessory," Brian Cavanaugh told his nephew, nodding at the baby in Dugan's arms. "It brings out the softer side of you." He turned toward Toni. "I take it this is your daughter."

Toni nodded. "This is Heather," she told the chief of Ds.

Brian put his index finger into the baby's tiny hand and smiled as Heather wrapped her little fingers around it.

"Nothing like a baby to make you realize what this is all about," he commented, his eyes smiling at the little girl. Then, looking at Toni, Brian told her, "You do very nice work, Ms. O'Keefe."

"Toni, please," she corrected him, then added, "Thank you."

She waited for the man to ask after the baby's father, but that didn't seem to matter to Brian. Her liking of the man increased.

Brian beckoned to an attractive blonde to come over to join them.

"Toni, I'd like you to meet my wife, Lila." There was pride in his voice as he told the younger woman, "These days, when she's not putting up with me, she heads the Missing Persons department."

"Then you're on the police force, too?" Toni asked the other woman.

"Is she ever," Brian laughed. "If it wouldn't insult all the other officers and detectives here, I'd say that Lila was the best damn police officer I ever had the pleasure to ride with."

These people were just one surprise after another, Toni thought. "You were partners?"

"We *are* partners," Lila answered, slipping her arm around her husband's waist. "It just took us a while to get together," she confided.

Toni looked at the woman. It occurred to her that these people constituted a treasure trove of unwritten stories. Her curiosity was completely aroused. "I'd love to sit down and talk to you sometime."

"Anytime," Lila told her.

The woman sounded genuine in her response, Toni couldn't help thinking.

"I'm going to steal Toni away because there are an awful lot more people to introduce her to," Dugan told the couple.

That seemed to be Heather's cue to start fussing.

Lila smiled, recognizing the sound. "She's hungry, isn't she?" she asked Toni.

"Probably," Toni answered. She began digging into the bag that was still hanging off Dugan's shoulder. Dugan shrugged it off to give her better access to the contents.

"Oh, please, let me," Lila said. "It's been a while since I got to do this sort of thing," she confided. "I really miss them when they're this age," she added with a fond smile.

Rather than surrender Heather, Dugan looked to Toni for permission.

Toni had no problem with it. If she couldn't trust the chief of Ds' wife, whom could she trust? "Please, go right ahead," she told Dugan, nodding toward the other woman.

"Oh, what a big girl you are," Lila cooed, expertly slipping her arms around the baby. "You're hungry, aren't you? Well, the bad news is that you can't have Andrew's pork loin today, but the good news is that once you get in some teeth and start eating solid food, you'll be able to eat his meals any time you want." Holding the baby, she turned toward Toni. "Would you mind if I gave Heather her bottle?"

"Not at all." Toni pulled out one of the three she'd packed before they left her house. "Here you go."

"Wonderful." Lila took the bottle in her free hand. "Go, mingle. Enjoy yourself. I'll take care of this little charmer," she told Toni.

Toni looked a little uncertain as she raised her eyes toward Lila. "Are you sure you don't mind?"

"Oh, I so don't mind," Lila assured her with enthusiasm. She looked at Dugan. "Give her the tour, dear. I think Toni could use the diversion."

"You heard the lady," Dugan said, carefully steering Toni toward the rear of the house.

Toni looked over her shoulder, still slightly concerned. But Lila looked as if she had everything under control. Satisfied that it was all right to leave Heather, at least for a bit, Toni gave herself permission to relax for a few minutes.

"You have an incredible family," she told Dugan as they went toward the backyard.

"I know. I've got to admit that, at times, they can get a little overwhelming. But they all mean well," he told her.

They were on the patio now. The backyard was unusually large, especially for the area. There were several tables set up, all with different appetizers on them. One table was devoted to beverages, both soft and hard.

"Would you like a drink? Or an appetizer?" he asked, giving her a choice.

"Appetizer," she told him. "I'm really not much for drinking these days," she admitted. "I had to give it up when I found out I was pregnant with Heather and for the most part, I never really got back into the habit." She flushed a little. "I probably sound awfully dull to you, don't I?"

"Dull? You?" he questioned with a laugh. "That is one word that I definitely wouldn't apply to you. Besides, drinking doesn't make someone exciting," he told her. "It's everything else that does."

His eyes washed over her for a moment and she felt a tingle that had nothing to do with anything they were talking about. She told herself that she was just imagining things. It had been almost a year since she'd been with anyone and she was just experiencing a longing for a little tenderness, nothing more.

"Fortunately for you," Dugan continued, "there're a lot of appetizers to choose from."

Her main concern was not food. She looked around at the gatherings of people. They seemed to be everywhere. Were they all family?

"There have to be at least fifty people here," Toni commented.

"More, actually," Dugan corrected. "Or, at least, more are coming," he amended. "We don't all come at the beginning and we don't all stay until the end, but we do all show up for at least a little while." When she looked at him, he explained, "Uncle Andrew's get-togethers are just too good to pass up."

"How can he afford to feed everyone like this?" she marveled, clearly amazed. "This kind of thing has to cost him a fortune, doesn't it?"

"Not quite," Dugan told her. "And we all pitch in. Sometimes more, sometimes less, but everyone foots some of the bill, giving what they can. And it's well worth it," he assured her. "Okay, enough background information," Dugan declared. "Let's get you introduced to at least some of the family."

"I'm not expected to remember everyone's name, am I?" she asked him. "I'm mean, I'm pretty good when it comes to names, but this is like—well, a crowd scene," she confessed.

Dugan started to laugh. When he finally caught his breath, he said, "Hell, no. I'm not even sure I remember everyone's name," he told her. "Although I'm pretty sure that Uncle Andrew probably not only knows everyone's names, he knows their middle names, as well—and probably their ages. But I don't," he repeated.

"That's because Cousin Dugan has a mind that bears a lot of resemblance to a sieve," Brianna O'Bannon told her, coming up behind the duo. She put out her hand to Toni. "Hi, I'm Detective O'Bannon," she said. "*Cavanaugh* O'Bannon," she specified. "My mother's a Cavanaugh. Maeve," she added for good measure, although she knew without saying that, at least for now, the journalist wasn't going to remember that piece of information. There was just too much to take in.

Toni felt overwhelmed. "I am going to need a scoreboard," she told Dugan.

"One will be provided for you on your way out," he told her with a completely straight face. And then he looked at Brianna. "Please, don't scare the woman off, Bri."

"Hey, I hear she came willingly," Brianna said, momentarily turning her attention back to Dugan. "Not like Jackson when it was his first time." She rolled her eyes. "I practically had to kidnap the man to bring him to one of these things," she confided to Toni. "The man actually had the audacity to say that he believed he was better off as a loner." She grinned. "Until the family got a hold of him, of course, and showed him the error of his ways," she added proudly. "That's him over there," she went on to say, pointing her fiancé out to the journalist. Jackson was standing over in a corner, talking to several other members of the family. "The guy with the big grin on his face."

"He's grinning like that because he thinks that you're busy elsewhere, so he's got a reprieve," Dugan told her. He pretended to shake his head. "Poor guy doesn't realize yet that you're about to come swooping back in his direction at any second."

Brianna looked at Toni. "You have my sympathy."

Toni read between the lines. "Oh. We're not a pair," she quickly told Brianna.

Bri merely smiled. She wasn't buying it. "Of course you're not," she answered. And with that, she went to join Jackson.

"Don't mind her," Dugan advised. "Ever since she and Jackson finally got together, she thinks everyone in the world should be paired off."

"She's right. They should be," a tall, dark-haired man said, coming up on Dugan's other side.

Dugan didn't even have to look to know who it was. "Toni, meet my cousin Bryce Cavanaugh," Dugan said. Because he knew word had gotten around about her, he jumped ahead of any question that Bryce might ask by saying, "Toni's the journalist who was at the restaurant when Michael Oren was killed."

"Yes, I did hear about that," Bryce confirmed. "And you still came out here after all that?" he marveled with a laugh. "I guess Uncle Andrew's reputation as a chef can really draw a person in. Hey, if you have any questions about anything—especially about this guy," he said, jerking his thumb in Dugan's direction, "Come see me. Oh, I think my wife's looking for me. We'll talk later," he told Toni just before he slipped away.

"Nice talking to you," Dugan called after his cousin, pretending to be slighted.

"Is everyone in your family this incredibly friendly?" Toni asked, amazed at how approachable everyone seemed to be. She couldn't recall ever meeting a group of people who came close to this sort of open, friendly behavior.

"No, actually, you just met the morose members," Dugan deadpanned. "C'mon," he coaxed. "Let's get you fed before everything disappears and we have to wait for the next wave of food."

She stared at him, trying to understand what he was telling her. "There are waves?" she questioned.

Dugan grinned. "Oh, lady, you are in for one hell of a treat," he promised her.

And she was, she discovered.

Not only was the food amazing, but she found that the conversation was even more so.

Although she had come here open and very willing to engage in conversation, she was amazed at the number of different conversations. There were all sorts of groups talking about all sorts of subjects. If one subject didn't interest her, there was another one that was guaranteed to absorb her.

Time seemed to slip by at an amazing rate.

Although Toni periodically stopped what she was doing and went in search of her daughter during the course of that day, there was always someone else asking to hold Heather or feed her or even, much to Toni's amazement, change the baby's diaper.

There was no end to the number of different women who were willing and even eager to take care of Heather for at least a few minutes. Usually longer.

And everyone was also more than willing to not just talk to Toni, but to answer her questions about past cases and present ones. It was like sharing an incredible pool of information.

"You're right," Toni said much later that evening. "You really do have an incredible family and I had an absolutely wonderful time meeting them. I loved the food, too," she quickly added as she packed up Heather's things. "It's hard to understand how you people aren't all overweight, what with all this fantastic food you eat. How *do* you stay so fighting trim?"

"Well, for one thing, we do a lot of chasing after bad guys," Shaw Cavanaugh, the precinct's newest chief of police as well as Andrew's son, said, having caught the tail end of her question. Like most of the family, he'd been introduced to her earlier. "I hope you didn't find any of my family intimidating," he told her.

"Intimidating?" she echoed, scoffing. "I want to find a way to be adopted by them. I always thought I was missing out by not coming from a large family, but now I'm completely convinced of it." Shaking her head, Toni looked at Dugan. "You people don't know how very lucky you are."

"Oh, I think we might have a clue," he assured her. "That's why we make a point of bringing people here with us. To share the wealth, so to speak."

"Was that why you had me come?" Toni asked.

"Among other reasons. But right now, I think you need to get this princess to bed," he said, indicating the baby, "so we'd better leave."

This, she thought as she prepared to take her leave of what was still a very crowded room, had been an experience she wasn't about to forget anytime soon.

# Chapter Sixteen

"I really did have a very good time," Toni said to Dugan more than an hour later as they drove back to her house.

It had taken them that much time to finally say all their goodbyes and just get into the car with the baby. Toni felt tired but happy at the same time. She really couldn't remember the last time she had been so all-around content about anything.

Turning toward Dugan now, she said, "Thank you for asking us to come along."

Dugan eased his car up against the curb in front of her house.

"Sure, any time," he told her. "Uncle Andrew holds these get-togethers pretty regularly. It used to be for an occasion, now it's just anytime he feels like getting everyone to come together. That's usually most months. I'll let you know the next time he decides to have one of these things."

"I think I'd like that," Toni told him.

There was no "think" about it. She knew she'd really like going back again. And not just for the stories or what she could eventually wind up writing about this amazing family. They had a way of making her feel completely included. It was an incredibly good feeling. It had been a long time since she'd felt as if she was part of a family. Not since her father died.

Getting out of the car, Toni began to take the baby seat out while Heather was still in it, but Dugan came around the front of the vehicle and moved her out of the way.

"Here, I'll do that," he told her.

She was about to say "No, I've got this," but decided that maybe she should just allow him to take over, at least for now. It was nice having someone help out once in a while. She did have Lucinda helping her with the baby, but that wasn't the same thing. Lucy did it out of a sense of gratitude, not just because she wanted to do it. It was somehow different with Dugan.

*Stop analyzing things. Just enjoy it, for heaven's sake.*

"Okay, got her," Dugan announced.

She took that as her cue and led the way to the front door. Pausing, she hit the keypad to disarm the lock. Opening the front door, she stepped inside and then, turning around to face him, took both the baby and the baby seat from Dugan.

Her eyes met his, but instead of telling him that he was free to go, she asked, "Would you like to come inside for a minute?"

Dugan looked at her for a long moment. She thought that he was going to take her up on her suggestion and come in.

Especially when he answered, "Yes."

She flashed a smile at him. "Good. I'll be right back. I'm just going to put the baby down for the night," she told him as she started to turn away.

"Which is why I'd better not," Dugan concluded honestly. She looked at him in surprise. "Don't get me wrong," he went on. "I want to, but that's exactly why I shouldn't. I don't think that would be such a good idea right now. We're working together and I don't want anything to compromise that," he explained.

That wasn't the real reason, but it was the simplest reason he could give her without making her realize that he was developing feelings for her. Real feelings.

She felt oddly deflated. "You're right," Toni agreed, forcing herself to sound as if she actually meant what she was saying. "Not that anything was going to happen," she added quickly, wanting him to understand that. "Two friends can have a drink and enjoy each other's company without anything having to happen," she told him firmly. "I'm sure that kind of thing goes on all the time—drinks between friends."

"All the time," he echoed. He had a feeling that she didn't believe that any more than he did. But that still didn't change the fact that he didn't want to get ahead of himself and do something that would cause either one of them—or both—to lose their focus—or get any further involved with each other. "I'll see you Monday."

"Monday," she echoed. "Oh, Dugan, wait a second," she called after him. As he turned back around to face her again, Toni placed the car seat on the floor. Heather mercifully continued sleeping.

"Yes?" he asked, waiting.

"Good night," she told him just a second before she caught hold of his lapels and kissed him.

Hard.

Just as he was about to succumb to his feelings and take her into his arms, she stepped back, laughter in her eyes. "See you Monday," she echoed. The next second, she'd eased him out the door and begun to re-arm her security system.

Dugan stood there for a moment, still feeling the imprint of her lips on his and the ripple effect it had had on his soul. He debated knocking on the door, asking her to let him back in.

And then he laughed, shaking his head to himself. That would really mess things up.

"Good night, O'Keefe," he said as he walked back to his car.

*Oh, wow,* Toni thought, her back against the wall. She slid down against it.

That had been hard.

As if on cue, Heather stirred, then began to wake up. The next second, she was making her displeasure known by crying. Toni recognized the sound. That was the baby's hungry cry.

Good, Toni thought. She needed something to take her mind off the evening that just might have been.

"So, how was it?" Lucinda asked her the following day as she came into the kitchen for coffee. "Should I stay in the guest room until he leaves?"

"No need," Toni told her as she made herself a slice of white toast. "The 'he' you're referring to left last night."

Lucinda was disappointed. "What happened?" she asked.

"Nothing happened," Toni answered. "I mean, not in the way you mean," she said, assuming that the young woman was referring to something having gone badly. "I had a great time," she stressed. "There was fantastic food and fabulous conversation and when it got late, Dugan brought us home."

Lucinda looked at her, trying to understand what Toni was telling her. "And then he left?"

"And then he left," Toni confirmed.

Lucinda frowned. Something was definitely off. "Tell me everything so I can tell you what you did wrong," she told Toni.

She loved the young woman dearly and at times really thought of her as family. But she didn't like anyone butting into her business.

"Lucy—"

"No, really," Lucinda insisted. "Something had to have gone wrong. He was really into you. I could see it in his eyes. You really need to get out there again. You don't want to wind up being just a career woman your whole life, do you?" Lucinda asked. "That's just living half a life."

"I'm not *just* a career woman," Toni reminded her. "I'm a mother. I have Heather, remember?"

"Which is another thing," Lucinda brought up. "Heather needs a dad. It doesn't have to be her own. Actually, she's probably better off if it's not her own. Any guy who'll walk out on you the second he finds out that you're pregnant—"

"Lucy, I appreciate your loyalty, but we're not having this conversation again," Toni informed her solemnly. She wasn't angry, but she was very serious. This was her business and it was not something she intended to hold an open forum about.

"You're right," Lucinda agreed. "We're not. We're going to talk about you going out with Mister Tall-dark-and-handsome," she insisted. "You've got to get your feet wet again—as well as other parts of your body," Lucinda added with a big grin.

Toni gave her a very serious warning look. "Lucy…"

But Lucinda took no heed. "The next time he brings you home, I'll just take Heather with me to my place. That way, you can have a mommy's night out—or in if you'd prefer," she added with a smile that needed no interpretation.

Toni threw up her hands. "I'm not having this conversation."

"No, but I am," Lucinda insisted. "You don't want to look back years from now and think of him as the one who got away, do you?"

"I don't want to look back at him at all," Toni lied. Just then, she heard a familiar noise. "Oh, thank God, the baby's crying. We'll talk later," she said, hurrying out to the baby's room.

"Count on it!" Lucy called after her.

When Dugan came in early the following morning, he immediately looked toward Toni's desk. She wasn't there. He felt his stomach sink like lead. A feeling of disappointment washed over him.

He'd left a police officer guarding her place, just in case Padilla showed up, although this was now just a precaution. Padilla was either dead or gone, Dugan was almost sure of it. No, Toni wasn't here for another reason. He wondered if she'd decided to take it slow after what had happened both Friday and then on Saturday—or if there was another reason she wasn't here.

Maybe she'd decided that this just wasn't worth it.

But that would make her a quitter, and he wasn't sure if he could really buy into that.

Just as he was attempting to come to terms with her absence, he saw Toni coming in. Not from the hallway, but from the back of the squad room. She was carrying a number of folders and they were up against her chest, making her look like an overworked student whose arms were loaded down with a large number of beige folders.

"You look surprised to see me," Toni commented. There was nothing she liked better than catching him off guard.

Dugan shrugged. "I thought maybe you'd decided you weren't coming in today."

"Why on earth would I decide not to come in?" she asked. "I've been researching our problem."

"Our problem?" he repeated, not sure just which problem she was referring to.

Maybe she'd just made that up to catch him by surprise, he thought. That was a distinct possibility, given the way she'd thrown him for a loop Saturday evening. If he tried, he could still taste her lips on his. He'd spent the rest of his weekend thinking about how he *might* have spent his Sunday if he'd acted on his initial reaction to her.

"The drug war," Toni specified. "I've been reaching out to some old contacts and—" She stopped when she saw the expression on his face. "Why are you smiling like that?"

If he told her that he was relieved to see her, or that she'd made a great impression on everyone Saturday, he wasn't sure how she would react. She might just take it to be a way of getting to her or to continue something that hadn't had a chance to play out. Yet.

But since she was already working full throttle ahead, he decided to just go with that and ask to be filled in on what she was thinking.

"Just glad it's Monday," he told her. "So, go ahead.

You were saying?" he coaxed, taking off his jacket and dropping it on the back of his chair.

"Turns out that Padilla might not have killed Oren because they belong to rival drug cartels," she told him. She could see that she'd caught him by surprise. "The killing might have been personal."

He took a breath, settling in. "Go ahead. I'm listening."

"Oren stole Padilla's girlfriend, then tossed her aside once he'd done what he wanted to with her. It's a very old story," she added.

"What a winner," Dugan commented, frowning.

She liked the fact that he didn't just disregard her theory as simply that. A theory. "I know, but this means that Padilla didn't kill Oren over routes or drug shipments or territory wars."

"Doesn't mean it can't escalate to that," Dugan pointed out.

She nodded. "I know, but right now, it still might just be about that. What I'm saying is that Padilla might not have his cartel covering his back over this, at least, not for the time being. So we could have an easier time getting to him," she said excitedly.

"Hold it," Dugan cried, putting his hands up to stop her narrative from going any further. "We?" he questioned skeptically.

"Well, yes," she told him. Then, because he was looking at her curiously, she specified. "You, your team. Me."

He shook his head. There was no way that he was about to consider putting her life in jeopardy.

"This is getting way too dangerous to bring you in, O'Keefe," Dugan told her.

She stared at him, dumbfounded. Was he kidding? "But I already *am* in. And anyway, it's actually less dangerous, not more," she told him. "We're after one guy, not a whole cartel."

"Yes," Dugan emphasized. "One guy *who you shot in the leg*," he underscored. "He's not about to forget that."

"If you get him without me, it doesn't matter what he doesn't forget," she said. "The point here will be that you did get him and, more than likely, Padilla will want to make a deal so that he doesn't spend the rest of three lifetimes in jail."

Dugan stared at her, dumbfounded. "Are you hearing yourself?" he asked.

"Yes," she answered. "And I think that not only do I like what I'm hearing, I think that the chief of Ds is going to like hearing it, too," she informed him with a confidence he found incredibly annoying. Because it might be true and it put her in danger. No matter how he sliced it, all he could think about was that she could get hurt.

Or worse.

He decided that the best thing he could do was to get her to back off.

"Look, they all liked you, but let's not get carried away here," he warned.

"They did?" she asked, her eyes suddenly wide. For all the world, she made him think of a little girl at Christmas. "They liked me?"

"Yes," he told her, winding down just for a moment. "They did. But they also know that getting a civilian involved in police business—"

"I'm not a civilian," she insisted. "I'm a professional."

"Journalist," Dugan underscored. "You're a professional *journalist*. That doesn't make you James Bond—or even Jane Bond," he told her, struggling hard to hang on to his temper.

"Look, I've undertaken a lot of dangerous assignments," she said. "And I still managed to make it to thirty-one. That's not just luck."

"Isn't it?" he challenged.

She knew what he was doing. He was trying to make her lose her temper. Toni hunkered down, instead. "I can certainly help you get this guy, too."

"How?" he asked. "How are you going to help us get this guy? By acting as bait?" Dugan demanded angrily.

She took a breath, steeling herself off. "If that's what it takes."

He threw his hands up. "Omigod! You, woman, are crazy." Taking a breath, Dugan forced himself to calm down. He needed to reason with her. "Besides, he's probably already left the country."

She wasn't convinced of that, not by a long shot. "From everything we know about him, Padilla has a vendetta mentality. The man's not going to be happy until he shoots me."

Dugan closed his eyes, shaking his head. "Fantastic."

"But I'll have you and your team watching me every step of the way," she insisted, trying to make him understand what she was thinking. "All we have to do is get him to come out and show his hand. And voilà, you've got him."

His eyes met hers. His were blazing. "No," Dugan bit off.

She pulled back her shoulders, bracing herself. "I can do it without you," she countered.

His eyes widened. "No, you can't," he said, refusing to believe that she would actually go through with something so dangerous.

"Wanna bet?" she asked in a low voice that, insanely, he found exceptionally sexy.

"Look, if I have to tie you up and keep you prisoner somewhere until this blows over, I will. Don't think I won't."

"I doubt that the chief will approve of that," she replied coolly.

"What he doesn't know won't hurt him—or me," he informed her.

"C'mon, Dugan," Toni coaxed. "You know that's not your style."

"Neither is putting your life in danger," he told her firmly.

She had to make him understand. "Dugan, my life's already in danger. That guy's out there looking for me and it's only a matter of time before he finds me. This way, we bring the war to him on our terms and you can protect me."

He was beginning to feel overwhelmed—and that

he couldn't get through to her. "Where do you even *get* these ideas?" he asked.

She grinned at him. "I read a lot," she told Dugan. "So, is it a deal? Are we going to do this together? Or are you going to make me wind up doing this all alone?" she asked, looking up at Dugan with her big, hopeful doe eyes.

"All right," he said, surrendering. "We'll do it your way," he ground out between clenched teeth. "But not without a lot of prep work being put into it first," he warned. "We're not going into this blind like we wound up doing last time."

"All right, you're the boss," she told him innocently.

"Ha!" was all Dugan allowed himself to say in response, at least for now.

# *Chapter Seventeen*

A week passed.

A week in which Toni went in, every day, expecting that *this* was going to be the day that she would be able to confront the man she knew wanted to eliminate her from the face of the earth.

Except that she didn't.

Despite a few sightings, Padilla was nowhere to be found.

Her life, Toni came to realize, had changed. Not because of the kind of work she did, not because she was part of something bigger than her ongoing story, but because she no longer did anything alone.

She had a bodyguard.

At first, maybe because she didn't quite believe it, she didn't fully realize she had one, because although he accompanied her home at the end of the day, Dugan left her on her doorstep.

Or so she thought.

She learned otherwise quickly enough. It actually happened several hours into the following day.

It was just a little after four in the morning. Heather had woken up for her first feeding and rather than just remain upstairs with her until the baby fell asleep again, Toni brought the little girl down and walked the floor with her for a while.

It wasn't quite light yet, but she was able to make out shapes clearly across the street.

When she saw the Mustang, at first Toni thought she was just imagining things. But a closer look told her that she wasn't. That was Dugan's vehicle.

And Dugan was sitting in it.

Surprised, Toni was about to go talk to him, then thought better of it. She was wearing a pair of cutoffs and a tank top, not the best attire to go waltzing across the street in, she decided.

Looking at the baby, she saw that Heather had fallen asleep.

She took the baby back upstairs to her crib. Putting her down, Toni stood there for a couple of seconds, making sure the baby didn't wake up. Heather went on sleeping, so she was free to hurry back down the stairs.

Toni looked out the window again just to make sure that the car was still there and that she hadn't conjured up the whole thing in her head. She hadn't. The car was still there.

*He* was still there.

She sighed, shaking her head. Why hadn't he said anything to her about this?

Picking up her phone from the table where she was charging it, she called Dugan's number. He answered her on the first ring.

Well, at least he wasn't asleep this time, she thought.

"Just what are you doing outside my door?" Toni demanded.

She saw him stretching. "Answering the phone," he told her.

*Idiot!* she thought. "Don't get wise with me, Cavanaugh."

"Oh, but I do it so well," Dugan quipped, looking out of his window toward her house. Seeing that she had the curtain pulled back, he waved at her.

She took a deep breath, reminding herself that losing her temper was not the way to go with this man. She tried to approach the subject reasonably. "Why didn't you tell me you were playing bodyguard again?"

"Well, for one thing," he told her, "the subject didn't come up—"

Okay, enough with being reasonable, she thought. "Dugan!"

"And, for another, I wanted to put off getting into this kind of a discussion with you for as long as possible."

Toni continued looking at him—and then sighed.

He was being protective of her. She really couldn't stay mad at him for that.

"Okay, get in here," she ordered.

"Why?" he asked suspiciously. "Do you have something sharp and pointy you want to stick into me?"

The absurdity of his question and the serious tone of voice that he asked it in totally disarmed her and she started to laugh. Any annoyance she had felt dissipated. "Just get in here, Cavanaugh."

"Yes, ma'am," he answered, pretending to go along with whatever she had in mind.

Dugan ended the call and she watched him get out of his vehicle. Within less than a minute, he had crossed the street to her house.

She moved over to the door. Hitting the keypad, she disarmed the alarm and let him in, then shut the door again behind him. She paused just long enough to rearm the security system before turned to confront him.

"This your idea?" she asked.

"In part." Then he quickly added, "The chief doesn't disagree."

"Fine." She liked feeling that she could take care of herself, but with Lucinda as well as Heather in the house, she supposed that she did appreciate the extra protection. "But if you're going to be Kevin Costner, you might as well sack out on my sofa."

She had lost him at the mention of the other man's name. "Say what again?"

"Kevin Costner," she repeated. When he still looked at her blankly, she prompted, "*The Body-*

*guard*," naming a popular film from 1992. She saw that it still made absolutely no impression on him. "Not an old movie buff," she realized. "Okay, never mind. That doesn't change the fact that if you're going to do this, you might as well not get a stiff neck sitting up all night in your car." She paused to look at him. "You really think I'm in any danger?"

He decided to be honest with her. "Yes, I do. But since I can't get you to back off and just disappear with your baby for a while until this is over, this is the next best thing I can do."

Toni sighed impatiently. She knew he was right. This had been her argument for getting Dugan and his team to let her stay to begin with.

Resigned, Toni asked the detective, "Can I get you anything?"

His eyes swept over her. Damn but she had an even better figure than he'd thought. The cutoff shorts and tank top fairly clung to her body—the way he would have liked to.

Dugan cleared his throat. "More clothes would be nice."

She looked at him, confused. "You want more clothes?"

"For you," he told her. "Because right now, what you've got on—or lack thereof—is a pretty big distraction."

And then she understood. She had begun to think that he only saw her as an assignment. Obviously not. She rolled the thought over in her mind. It pleased her a great deal.

"Why, detective, is that compliment?" she asked, grinning.

"That is an observation," he told her solemnly, leaving it at that.

"And it's a lovely one, too," she said, pleased. It was nice to know that she wasn't the only one who felt an attraction between them. "You want a blanket?" she asked, nodding at the sofa. "Or maybe a cup of coffee?"

"Coffee. Black—if you already made it," he added quickly. He didn't want her going to any extra trouble on his account.

"I haven't, but it'll only take a second," she told him. "And then you can tell me what you have planned for today—besides taking a cat nap sometime, of course," she added.

"What made you look outside?" he asked her, raising his voice as she crossed into the kitchen. And then the answer suddenly occurred to him before she said anything. "Are you worried that someone followed you?" he asked. Had Toni seen anyone who shouldn't have been there?

"I didn't think about that," Toni answered. "No. I guess it was just a gut feeling I had," she admitted. Toni heard him laugh. "What's so funny?"

"That's a Cavanaugh stock answer," he told her. "Every time one of our moves are questioned, we usually say we did what we did because we had a gut feeling."

"I'll have to remember that," Toni called back.

"As for me," she told him, "I've had gut feelings as far back as I can remember."

"Have they ever been right?" Dugan asked.

Toni came back into the living room, a steaming cup of coffee in her hand. She stood before him, looking at Dugan for a long moment before finally answering.

"Actually, most of the time," she told him.

He took the coffee cup from her. "That was quick," he noted.

"I have one of those instant brew machines. It practically makes the coffee the minute you think of having a cup," she said. And then she glanced at her watch. "You know, it's only a little after four. Why don't you grab a little shut-eye while you still can?" she suggested. "I'll just get out of your way and go back upstairs. I promise not to flee or do anything bad until at least after six o'clock in the morning." She crossed her heart for emphasis.

He didn't think he could get any sleep right now. He waved her off. "Do whatever it is you normally do. Pretend I'm not here."

*Easier said than done, Detective Cavanaugh,* Toni thought as she left the room and went back up the stairs to her room.

It got a tiny bit easier after that, but not much. And the waiting, the expectation, just grew that much harder.

Twice during the week that followed, she thought

they had Padilla, only to discover that either the report was false or they had just missed him.

Whether he was lucky, or just that good, the drug lord continued to elude them.

They had a little more success when it came to tracking down the actual delivery date of the next drug shipment. Although plenty of false leads had been planted, one by one those were weeded out.

They were getting closer.

However the continuing follow-ups and the waiting were beginning to take a real toll on her nerves. Dugan could see it in her face even though she wasn't saying anything.

"You know, you can bail anytime you want," Dugan told her in his car, not for the first time.

She was *not* about to do that, and if he thought she was, Toni thought, the man was crazy. "The only thing worse than dealing with all these false leads is sitting home, *hearing* about all these false leads. At least this way I'm doing something. If I were just sitting at home, waiting for you to tell me it's over, I'd be slowly going crazy."

She was forgetting about something, Dugan thought. "What about Heather?"

Toni shrugged. "She's too busy being a baby to notice anything going wrong at this stage."

He frowned at her. "No, I meant wouldn't you be busy taking care of her? Wouldn't that be enough to keep you busy?" he asked. His association with Toni and her baby had quickly educated him as to how much attention a baby really required.

"Babies are a lot of work," she told him, knowing that was the point he thought he was making. "But there's a lot of downtime in between those work periods," she pointed out. "I don't do downtime well," she confided. "I'm more like you. I'm a doer."

There had to be something she could do other than put herself in the path of danger. "What about your work?" Dugan reminded her. "You could write."

She knew he meant well, but the man obviously didn't understand.

"I'm an investigative journalist, Cavanaugh," she reminded him. "There's not much to investigate if you're confined to the house with a three month old. Besides," she continued. "If I were home, you'd want me to stay home until you catch Padilla, right?"

There was no point in telling her she was wrong. "You're right, I would," he answered. He pulled into her driveway. He could see that his presence seemed to irritate her. It was the last thing he wanted to do. "Look, if you'd rather have someone else as your bodyguard, I understand."

"Well, you might, but I don't." She turned in her seat to get a better look at him. "Why would I want someone else guarding Heather and me? After all, you packed your bag and everything," she pointed out with a big smile. "Can't let all that packing go to waste, now, can I?"

He looked at her, exasperated by her attitude as well as happy that she hadn't agreed that she'd be better off with someone else guarding her. "You know what I mean."

"Nope, sorry, I don't." She gazed into his eyes, daring him to prove her wrong.

"Okay, never mind," he told her, surrendering. Dugan got out of the vehicle. "Let's go see what Lucinda made for dinner tonight."

Toni got out on her side. "Lucy loves cooking for you, you know. She likes the compliments that you pay her."

He didn't see why that was such a big deal. "Well, the food's good," Dugan pointed out. "Why shouldn't I tell her that I like it?"

She could only laugh as she shook her head. There were times that the man was incredibly innocent.

"You have no idea how rare that is. I mean, I tell her something's good, but that doesn't make an impression because she feels I'll say that even if she serves up three-day-old shoe leather. You, on the other hand, well, you're a guy."

"Thank you for noticing," he commented dryly.

"My point," she stressed as they walked up to the front door, "is that guys don't usually notice things like that. She had three brothers and not one of them ever had anything good to say about her cooking."

He tried to come up with a reason. "Maybe they just thought it was understood. Some people are uncomfortable giving compliments," he told her.

"True," Toni agreed. "But other people are just brainless dolts. I think her brothers fall into the latter category," she told Dugan. Even as the words were out of her mouth, she realized why he wouldn't have even thought of that. "You wouldn't understand that because your family's perfect."

*"Ha!"* was Dugan's immediate response. "They're not perfect. Not by a long shot."

She knew she could argue that point, but she decided to let it go for now. Dugan knew how lucky he was. No reason to belabor that thought.

"Okay, for the sake of argument, just let me put it this way. Your family is a lot more perfect than most families," she told him.

"Who's a lot more perfect?" Lucinda asked as she walked into the room, bringing Heather with her. She paused by the playpen and put the baby down in it. "By the way, dinner's going to be delayed. Her royal highness decided she was staying up longer and needed more attention."

"I'm fine with that," Dugan said. He walked over to the playpen and scooped the baby up into his arms. "Nothing like coming home to a baby at the end of another long, frustratingly unproductive day," he declared. Just holding her in his arms seemed to make him feel better. "Hi, sunshine, so how was your day? Was it good?" he asked.

Heather gurgled as if she was actually responding to his question.

Dugan laughed. "You don't say? It was that good, huh? Maybe you and I should trade days tomorrow. I'll stay and hang around here while you can go in and pretend you're me."

Toni looked at him, her eyes taking the measure of both the detective and the baby he was holding in his arms. "I think they might notice the height difference," she commented.

Dugan held the baby up, pretending to examine her from all sides. "You think there's a height difference? Where?"

"Lucy, I think the detective might need a drink tonight to make things clearer for him," Toni told the other woman.

"Naw," Dugan said, waving away Toni's suggestion. "All I need is right here, isn't it, doll-face?" he said, asking the baby for her input.

Heather gurgled again, as if to agree.

# Chapter Eighteen

"What if you never get Padilla?" Toni asked Dugan out of the blue several days later.

Their lives had taken on a certain routine now. They left together in the morning and came home together at night—her home, not his. Occasionally, Dugan would swing by his place to get his mail or another change of clothing, but even then, they always wound up at her house. She had even taken to doing his laundry along with her own, the baby's and Lucinda's.

In a way, at least temporarily, they had become a family of sorts. But she didn't want to get accustomed to this, accustomed to having him around, which was why she asked the question now.

"We'll get him," Dugan told her, sounding completely confident.

They were alone in the living room. Dinner was long over and the dishes had been cleared away. Lucinda had put the baby down and then gone to bed herself. The house felt oddly quiet right now.

So quiet that Toni could almost hear herself think, and her thoughts were disquieting.

She found herself looking forward to each day because she and Dugan would be together and the feeling did make her wary. She already knew she couldn't depend on having a man in her life. Heather's father was proof of that.

"But what if you don't?" Toni pressed. "Are you planning on being my bodyguard for the rest of my life?"

He looked at her, trying to understand where she was going with this. Was she just feeling him out, or was there a note of hostility in her voice?

"Would that be so bad?" he asked, watching her.

"Well, sure," Toni said. "For you," she added, watching him to see his reaction.

"Are you trying to get rid of me, Toni?" Dugan asked her, his voice sounding a little silkier than it normally did.

"Of course not," she told him, her eyes still on Dugan, "I just hate being a burden."

He waved away the thought. "Well, you're not."

But she wasn't about to let that go just yet. "Sure I am. You don't get to be you at the end of the day.

You're too busy guarding me, being alert," she stressed.

Dugan gave her another take on it. "Well, maybe that *is* me."

She wasn't buying it. "No, it's not. The first time I met you—the night you helped deliver Heather— you were coming back after a night of celebrating something at Malone's. Malone's is where you go to unwind and hang out. Malone's is also the place you haven't gone to since you started this side detail of 'guarding Toni.'"

He weighed his words carefully, not wanting to give too much away, but wanting to negate what she seemed to believe.

"Look, if I had a problem with this assignment, someone else would be spelling me. But the truth of it is…" He paused for a moment, gauging her response. "I feel better being the one who's looking out for you. I don't trust anyone to do a better job of guarding you than me."

His eyes were on hers. He was standing too close to her again, Dugan thought, upbraiding himself. That had been happening a lot these last couple of days. It was almost as if he was secretly daring himself to see how close he could get to her and still be able to reel himself back in without having done anything.

Without acting on his feelings.

It was, he thought, getting harder and harder for him.

"If I do have any problem with this," he continued,

his mouth suddenly feeling as if he'd tried to swallow a large wad of cotton, "it's—oh, hell, never mind."

"No, finish what you were about to say," Toni insisted, getting in his way as Dugan tried to turn from her.

He was deliberately trying to put some distance between them. His impulses were becoming more difficult to sublimate. Did she always wear that perfume? Because right now, it was filling his head.

Turning away again, he told her, "It's not worth finishing."

"Yes, it is," Toni insisted. She followed him across the room, then put her hand on his shoulder, forcibly turning him around. "Now tell me, what were you going to say?"

His eyes narrowed. "You're in my space," he told her gruffly.

If he meant to intimidate her, he wasn't about to succeed, Toni thought. She'd seen the man beneath that harsh facade, beneath that bluster. She'd seen the man who delivered her baby, the man who talked to Heather as if she were a cognizant tiny human being. That wasn't the kind of man given to focusing only on himself and not on anyone else.

She didn't want him turning away or hiding behind words. She wanted him to *really* talk to her, to tell her what was on his mind. There was something buzzing between them and she wanted it to become clearer, not disappear under a barrage of grunts and double-talk.

"I noticed," Toni acknowledged. "And I'm not

about to back off until you finish telling me what you started to say."

He lifted his shoulders in a vague, careless shrug. "I lost my train of thought," he told her.

Rather than backing off, the way he thought she would, Toni dug in.

"Then let me help," she offered. "You said that if you did have any problem with this assignment, it was because—" She looked up at him. "Now you fill in the blank."

He could almost *feel* her presence against him. Feel himself losing this battle he was unsuccessfully trying to wage. Annoyance bubbled up within him.

"Damn it, woman, I'm only a man."

He saw the smile that came into her eyes. "I'm not complaining."

He knew he should just push her away, but he couldn't get himself to do that. But maybe if he warned her, he could get her to back off on her own.

"If you don't let me put any distance between us, Toni," he told her, "I might not be responsible for what happens."

Toni caught her lip between her teeth, never taking her eyes off him. "And that would be...?" she asked breathlessly.

Hell, if he couldn't verbally get her to back off, he was just going to have to frighten her away. Taking hold of her shoulders, he shortened what was already practically a nonexistent space between them. Pulling her to him, Dugan kissed her.

Not with the sort of tenderness he might have exhibited if this was any other situation, but roughly, so that she would finally understand what was going on here and run for her life.

But a funny thing happened when he kissed her, Dugan discovered. She wasn't frightened away. She didn't come to her senses and run. Instead, Toni reacted exactly the way she had in his fantasy.

She kissed him back.

Her arms went around his neck, her body pressed against his and she kissed him with every fiber of her being. Kissed him as if this was the very first time she'd ever kissed anyone and she didn't want it to end. Ever.

Toni took his breath away, and in that moment, she managed to also do away with his defenses, reducing him to a mass of pulsating desire and burning passion.

It took a great deal of willpower for Dugan to force himself to break off the kiss and pull back from her. He very nearly didn't make it, but the training he had gone through as a police officer and then a detective provided him with the inner fortitude and the background he needed in order to pull it off.

Stepping back, he created the opening between them that allowed him to clear his head. In very short order, she had managed to fill every part of him with a longing he found next to impossible to control.

Slightly disoriented, she looked up at him. Why had he pulled away? "What's wrong? Don't you want to kiss me? Because if you don't, then I'll back off and—"

*Don't you want to kiss me?*

She had to be kidding. It was all he thought about every moment of every day when he wasn't forcing himself to think about the case.

The last bit of resistance he had completely crumbled. He knew every reason he shouldn't be doing this, why, if he was thinking straight, he should go back to his car and guard her from a distance.

But he wasn't thinking straight and none of that mattered.

All that mattered was this incredible desire that he'd been trying to dam up since the first moment he'd laid eyes on her. The desire that had broken through his reinforcements and come pouring out, rushing like a raging river that had finally been allowed to run free.

Catching her up in his arms again, Dugan began kissing her with feeling, as if his very soul depended on it.

The more he kissed her, the more intense his desire for her became.

This time, when they came up for air, she was the one to put the brakes on, at least for that moment.

"Not here," she breathed.

He understood.

Taking her hand, he led the way up the stairs to her bedroom. Once they reached it, Dugan had barely closed the door before she was back in his arms, her mouth sealed to his.

He kissed her over and over again, only marginally aware that they were taking each other's clothes off as his lips devoured her.

They found their way from the door to her bed, although that, too, wasn't a totally conscious process.

The only thing Toni was actually aware of was just how much she wanted him.

Yes, she'd been attracted to him and, yes, there had been this latent desire to discover what it would be like to be with him in the most intimate of ways. But she had no idea that once she began to explore she would feel as if she had been set on fire. A fire that was all-consuming and not only wouldn't let up, but just grew larger.

Everything she did only made her want him that much more.

She kissed Dugan's mouth, his neck, his face, working her way down along his upper torso, thrilling herself with every indulgence, every step forward she took. As she was getting totally caught up in feasting on him, suddenly he caught her hands in one of his, immobilizing her and holding her prisoner.

Toni blinked, looking at him, confusion in her eyes. "What?"

"You can't have all the fun," he whispered against her ear, his breath stirring her as it glided along her skin. And, just like that, he became the aggressor.

His hands and lips were passing over her body, anointing her, marking her, taking inventory of all of her as he made her twist and turn against him.

She bit her lip to keep from moaning. The nursery and the guest room were both clear down the hallway, but she didn't want to take a chance on waking Lucinda up. What was happening between the two of them was far too gloriously private for her to share with anyone else, even a person she regarded like a sister.

This—and he—were hers alone and she intended to keep it that way.

The sound of her heavy breathing filled the air as he brought her up to higher and higher plateaus of heart-racing enjoyment until she was afraid that she was going to lose control and cry out from the sheer ecstasy of what she was experiencing.

Somehow, although she really wasn't sure how, Toni managed to keep from screaming out her reaction.

But even so, she did her best to have him feel the very same building desire, to find himself tottering on the brink of almost excruciating, mind-numbing ecstasy.

Catching her hands, Dugan held them above her head as he moved his body slowly and seductively along hers, bringing her closer and closer to the uplifting crescendo her whole body was throbbing to experience. She felt herself hungering to feel that final wondrous moment and could hardly keep herself in check.

Arching her back, she moved against him, tempting him to take her.

"Look at me," he whispered hoarsely.

She realized that her eyes had shut in anticipation. Opening them now, she looked at him, her breath catching in her throat.

"Better," he told her.

His eyes held hers as he slowly entered her, then he sealed their mouths together before the final ascending dance began.

His hips moved slowly, then faster, increasing the tempo with each passing second.

Her heart pounded wildly as they continued to goad one another on until, finally, they captured the utmost peak, causing wild explosions to overtake them, shaking the very foundations of this world that they had created for just the two of them.

This time, she would have cried out his name if he hadn't sealed his mouth to hers at the very last moment. He had anticipated her.

Toni felt her head swirling when he finally drew back and then slid off her body.

Dugan gathered her to him and held her body against him, his heart still pounding, threatening to break out of his very chest.

It took him more than a few moments to recapture his breath and a few more before he was able to begin to breathe normally.

He felt her laughing against his chest and he looked at her quizzically. "What?"

"You guard everyone this closely?" she asked, her eyes all but dancing as she watched him.

"Only a special few," he replied solemnly.

"Oh?" She shifted so that her head rested on his chest. "How few?"

He thought a moment. "I can count them on one finger of one hand."

Toni propped herself up on her elbow and looked

at him more closely. "You're telling me that you've never done this before?" she asked, her tone ringing with skepticism.

"Oh, I've done this before," he told her. "Just never with someone I'm supposed to be guarding. You're the first in that category."

She smiled at him. He could feel her smile against his chest. "I'm glad."

"Well, I'm not," he answered. When she raised her head to look at him, he said, "I'm supposed to have more willpower than that."

For a moment, she'd thought he was telling her he had regrets about this, but now she understood what he meant. Her smile grew wider.

"Haven't you heard, Cavanaugh?" she asked. "I'm irresistible."

He sighed. "Just my luck."

"Yes," she answered, moving so that she wound up all but looming over him. "Just your luck," she repeated, lowering her mouth to his.

"Hey, wait a second," he said, taking hold of her face and holding her back. "You're going to have to give me a minute here. I'm good, but I'm not exactly superhuman, you know."

"No? Are you sure?" she asked, nipping his lower lip playfully before drawing back. "You could have fooled me." She kissed him again, then once again drew back. "How long do you think this revitalizing process is going to take?" She lowered her hand so that her fingertips began stroking him with slow, deliberate movements. "An hour? Thirty minutes?

Or maybe a little less than that?" she teased, her eyes laughing at him.

He caught her hand and pulled her back. "Maybe less than that."

There was mischief in his eyes a second before he brought his mouth down on hers again.

"Oh, you definitely are ready," Toni murmured, her arms encircling his neck.

## Chapter Nineteen

Another week went by, and then part of a third. Toni told herself not to get accustomed to having Dugan around, but it was really hard for her not to. Not when they wound up in bed together each night, seeking shelter in each other's arms.

Every morning she promised herself not to go on the way she had, to put on the brakes because it was preparing herself for a time when Dugan would tell her that he had to be moving on. A time that she knew, in her heart, was inevitable.

But each night, she whispered to herself "Just one more time," and then she made love with Dugan all over again.

Just when it was beginning to seem as if every tip regarding the Juarez Cartel's latest proposed shipment had dried up, Dugan took a phone call. At the end of it, he hung up the receiver on the phone on his desk and all but shouted, "I think we just got lucky!"

Toni looked up immediately. Up until this point, she had been going over her notes for what seemed like the dozenth time, searching for something they—Dugan, his team and she—might have overlooked, some clue that had gotten hidden beneath a blanket of rhetoric.

She asked the first thing that popped into her head. "You found Padilla?" Toni was already halfway out of her seat.

Excited over the information that had just come in via a very reliable informant, Dugan played back his own words in his head. He realized how they must have sounded to the woman he'd been guarding and for a moment was almost apologetic.

"Not that lucky," he amended. "Nguyen just called to say that his man's gotten wind of a shipment coming in by tomorrow via one of several newly discovered underground tunnels."

Detective Jason Nguyen had finally been cleared for work. Chomping at the bit to get back into the game and be productive, he'd begun rattling all the cages of every informant he knew.

Apparently, it had finally paid off.

"*By* tomorrow, not tomorrow," Toni repeated, looking at Dugan.

He could see that she understood the difference. "Right. That means that we've got to get people posted watching half a dozen tunnels, all of them running around three quarters of a mile underground from somewhere outside the city, ending in shacks and houses practically in the middle of nowhere."

She knew that there were over a thousand such tunnels honeycombing key delivery points. Most were in Mexico, some ran between Mexico and either California or Arizona. However, most were nowhere near where she and Dugan presently were.

"Aren't these things usually built near the border and coming into the US from there?" Toni asked.

"Well, for one thing, our cartel friends have gotten very creative," he told her. "They playing a game of musical drugs these days. They like keeping us and the Mexican government guessing and these underground tunnels make transportation safer and efficient."

"Speaking of guessing," Toni said, picking up on the key word. "Are we sure about this?"

Dugan shrugged. "Nothing is ever sure," he answered honestly. "But it's as sure as it can be, given that everyone involved on both ends of this transport is given to lying and would be more than willing to sell their mother for the right price."

Listening to him, Toni just shook her head. "We have *got* to get you to start hanging out with a better class of people."

For half a second, Dugan wasn't a narcotics detective, he was just a man trying hard not to fall in love with the woman he took to bed every night.

But he couldn't help smiling at her. "I do, remember?"

"Right. That family of cops that are backing you up," Toni deadpanned. And then she grew serious. She didn't want to think that what he was saying had any hidden meaning because it only meant getting *really* disappointed at the end of this. "Do you think that if this tip is on the level, it's enough to bring Padilla and his people out, as well? If they can steal this from the Juarez Cartel, then that would put them on top again, right?"

"Ultimately," Dugan admitted, "that's what I'm hoping for. If this doesn't draw Padilla out, it will at least attract some of his people. Maybe someone within his organization is looking to score a coup and take over the top position. That might mean that Padilla's on his way out. Without his people, Padilla will be easier to catch."

She studied his face. "Do you honestly believe that?"

Dugan spread his hands wide. "I'm an optimist. It's required in my family," he told her. "So, yes, I believe that if all the blocks fall into place the way we hope they do, we'll be in a better position to catch that SOB and put him away once and for all."

"Okay, you sold me," she told him. Retracing her steps back to her desk, she got her purse out of the drawer. "Let's get started."

He was on his feet, gesturing her down a notch or two. "Whoa, whoa, whoa, let's get started?" he questioned.

Had she suddenly stopped speaking English? "Yes, let's see if we can figure out which of these underground tunnels is going to be used so we can be waiting for them when they make their appearance like gophers popping out of their hole."

"*We're* not going anywhere," Dugan informed her, putting her off before she really got going. "Where did you get the idea that you were coming with me?" he asked.

How could he ask that? "Because I've gone everywhere else with you," she answered, puzzled by his question. Why was this any different from all the other times?

"That was when we were laying groundwork, getting information, looking for informants," he told her. He had wanted to keep her close then, but it was different now. He wanted to insure that she was safe and being with him wouldn't make her safe.

"Right," she agreed, trying to understand why Dugan would change his mind. She came up empty. "And this is where all that groundwork is finally paying off, right?" she challenged.

"For the department, yes," he agreed, then told her, "For you specifically, no." Couldn't she see how dangerous all this actually was? "This is not some Sunday walk in the park, Toni. These are dangerous people involved in this."

"I know that," she retorted angrily. "I'm not an idiot."

He followed that line of thinking. "Then you know that you have to stay home."

She sighed. "Well there you've lost me," Toni told him. She tried to make him understand what she was thinking. "I've been doing dangerous assignments since long before I met you."

"Well, now you have met me, and I'm not about to risk your life no matter how you phrase your request," Dugan told her, struggling not to lose his temper. "Don't you get it, Toni?" he demanded. "You *shot* Padilla. This guy wants you dead. I'm not about to let him get his wish by serving you up on a platter so that he'll be able to get off a clear shot at you."

She was losing her temper. "You just said he might not even be there—"

"But his people are bound to be," Dugan pointed out. "The payoff's too big to ignore and I'd bet my soul that his people all have orders to kill you."

"Padilla's an egomaniac. He'd want to take the shot himself."

Dugan's mouth almost dropped open. "You just made the damn argument for me," he retorted.

"No," she contradicted, "I just made the argument against my being at home like some damn sitting duck, waiting to be executed."

"I've got police officers watching your house, remember?" he reminded her. "Lucinda's even started to complain about it," he reminded her. "Said she felt like a prisoner in her own home—or more to the point, in your home."

Toni could see that he was serious and not about to give in. She couldn't let him win this. "Dugan, please. I can't just sit home and twiddle my thumbs, waiting to hear from you. I'll be climbing the walls within twenty minutes, especially since you don't even know when this shipment is actually coming— or exactly where. You've got more than a twenty-four-hour window here," Toni pointed out, frustrated.

He would have given in if he could, but this was her life they were talking about and the thought of doing without her, he'd suddenly realized, scared the hell out of him. So he remained strong and said no to her.

"Well, you're going to have to learn how to twiddle," he told her.

"I'll hate you," she threatened him.

"But you'll be alive to do it and that'll be okay with me," he told her.

"Dugan, please," she begged, all but disarming him with the look in her eyes.

He deliberately focused above her head because the expression in her eyes all but shredded him apart.

"Sorry, my mind's made up. I'd taking you home and that's that." He took hold of her shoulders, desperate to make her understand why he was doing this. "Look, if I'm worried about you, I'll be distracted. That's never a good thing on the job. It's liable to get me killed," he said bluntly. "If I know you're home, safe, all I have to look out for is myself. I can handle that. Now, do I make myself clear?" he asked, finally looking into her eyes.

"Abundantly," Toni answered, her voice all but dead and cold.

"Good." He knew she was far from happy, but he

wasn't about to press the matter. All he wanted was for her to be safe. If she ultimately hated him for it, so be it. "Patterson, you get the rest of the team and get on out to Pescadero. Tell them I'll be there as soon as I can. We'll split up from there."

"You got it, Cavanaugh." The other detective was already out the door.

The next thing Dugan did was place a call, ordering that the guard around Toni's house be doubled. When he hung up, he could see that she was still just as upset as ever. He had a feeling it was going to take her a long time to forgive him. But, as he'd told her, he could live with that because it meant that she *was* alive.

"Okay," he said, "let's go."

She fell into place beside him without uttering a single word.

"I have a bad feeling about this," Toni finally said ten minutes later as he drove her home.

*Finally!* he thought, she was talking to him.

"It should be over within the next twenty-four to thirty-six hours," Dugan estimated.

Toni shot him a dark look. "I'm not talking about that. I'm saying that I've got a gut feeling this is all wrong."

"Oh, right. I forgot about your gut feelings," Dugan said. There was just a touch of sarcasm in his voice.

"You're a Cavanaugh," she reminded him, her

voice formal and cool. "You're not supposed to discount a gut feeling."

"I'm not," he answered. "But you're *not* a Cavanaugh and that means that you can't fall back on that particular excuse."

"You need me," Toni insisted.

"That is beside the point," Dugan said, the look in his eyes telling her that he *did* need her, but he couldn't allow that to cloud his judgment. "I want you home, safe." He thought of the baby he'd helped deliver. "You haven't spent too much time with Heather in the last few weeks. Spend some time with her now."

"I don't need you to tell me when I should spend time with my daughter," she informed him coldly. "Heather is doing fine, which is more than I can say for her mother," Toni added angrily. "Look," she cried, trying one last time to talk him into taking her. "You won't have to protect me. I know how to use a gun and I promise I won't get in your way. I just want to be there with you because…because…"

"Because?" he prompted impatiently, waiting for her to finish.

"Because if anything happened to you and I wasn't there, I'd never forgive myself!" she snapped.

"But if I died in your arms, you'd be okay with that?" he challenged.

It was a ridiculous thing to say and he was well aware of that, but he wasn't feeling very reasonable at the moment.

"Damn it! That's not what I meant Cavanaugh and you know it!" she shouted at him.

"Yes, I know it," he shouted back. Taking a deep breath, he made himself calm down. This was *not* the way he wanted to leave her. "And I'm not going to die, so stop worrying."

Her eyes were blazing. "You can't know that."

He pulled up in front of her house. From where he sat, he could see the squad cars he'd asked for. They were parked at both ends of the block so they could see anyone coming from either direction.

"No, you're right. I can't. All I can do is my damndest to make sure that I come out of this alive. I'm working with some pretty good men and this isn't our first rodeo. Look," he took her hands in his, "I appreciate you worrying about me. I really do. But this is my job. It's what I do for a living and I'm good at it, even if I do say so myself. Besides…" His eyes all but caressed her. "I've got a lot to live for."

"Oh, God," she cried, "that's what the hero always says just before everything goes all wrong and blows up on him."

His mouth curved. "Well, at least I'm a hero," he quipped.

"You're an idiot," Toni countered in total frustration.

"A hero–idiot," Dugan repeated, pretending to roll that over in his mind. "How does that work?"

Toni didn't answer his question, instead, she told him, "I am going to worry about you the entire time, you know that, don't you?"

"I will be back before you know it," Dugan assured her.

She rolled her eyes. "That is a stupid, stupid line."

"Sorry. It's the best I've got," he answered. Then, before she could say anything more or argue with him, he pulled her into his arms and kissed her long and hard with every fiber of his being.

"That is going to have to hold both of us until I get back," he told her. "Now, c'mon, I'll walk you to your door and then I've got to go."

"If I'm so safe here, why do you have to walk me to my door?" she asked him, not attempting to hide the sarcasm in her voice.

Dugan sighed. "Because I'm a masochist."

Getting out, he rounded the hood and made his way to the passenger door. He opened it and she just continued sitting in the car.

"C'mon, Toni," he sighed. "Don't make this harder than it is."

"Why not?" she asked, then said, "You obviously are."

"We'll argue about this when I get back," Dugan told her.

Then, because she still wasn't moving, he reached into the vehicle and took her arm. She knew that he was a great deal stronger than she was, even if she dug in and refused to budge. Dugan would still be able to pull her out of the car and she didn't really want to cause a scene out here. Because if she did, that meant that she would be behaving too much like a petulant child and that wasn't what this was all supposed to be about.

This was about her wanting to be there with him when he captured the drug shipment, which she firmly believed that he would. And she wanted to be there just in case Padilla was there with the shipment because she was confident that Dugan would protect her.

But if he couldn't understand any of that, then there was no way that she could make him.

So, just as he took a better hold of her arm, she surrendered and slid out of the passenger seat on her own.

"All right, you win. I'm out of the car. I'll go into the house and cower in the corner somewhere until you come back and give the all-clear signal," she ground out between clenched teeth.

"You're being silly now," he told her as they walked up to the front door.

"No, I'm being obedient now. Isn't that what you want?" she challenged. "For me to be obedient?"

"What I want," he told her, "is for you to be understanding. And when you finally calm down, you will be. But for now, I don't have any more time to argue with you about this."

"So go," she told him.

He looked at the door. "Just as soon as you lock the door behind you."

"Don't insult me," she told him. "I know how to lock my door and rearm the security. Go!" she all but yelled at him. "Go be the hero and try not to get yourself shot. I don't like damaged goods."

"I'll remember that," he told her.

Because she had made him late as well as crazy, Dugan hurried away.

# *Chapter Twenty*

Toni deliberately stood in front of the door, watching Dugan until he got back into his car. She remained standing there until he pulled away. And then she finally disarmed the security alarm and let herself into her house.

She was still angry at him.

She felt exactly like someone's little sister who wasn't being allowed to tag along to the big party. Toni knew all the reasons she was being kept from going with him, and on an intellectual level, she grudgingly had to admit that she understood them.

But just because she understood them didn't make her feel any better, didn't change the fact that she was furious at Dugan because she had been deliberately excluded from this phase of the operation. She didn't like being left behind this way.

She fisted her hands at her sides, wanting to pummel something.

Maybe if she was angry enough at Dugan she wouldn't immediately dissolve into a mass of nerves and worry about him. Because he had sentenced her to spend the next day or so wondering if he and his team had found the right tunnel. And it didn't end there, because if they *did* manage to find the right tunnel, one or both of the cartels might show up to wage war over the drugs. Worrying about *that* would drive her completely out of her mind.

With a huge sigh, she engaged the security system. "Lucy, are you home?" she called out.

Within moments, Lucinda came walking into the room, emerging out of the kitchen. She looked surprised and perplexed to see Toni there in the middle of the day.

"What are you doing back here at this hour?" Lucinda asked, looking around the room. "Is your detective with you?"

"He's not *my* detective," Toni snapped. "Sorry," she apologized. She shouldn't be taking it out on the other woman.

"Uh-huh. Trouble in paradise?" Lucy asked. She eyed Toni closely. "What did you do?"

"I didn't do anything," Toni answered sharply, annoyed at Lucinda's assumption. "Not a damn thing."

Lucinda looked at her doubtfully. "Then why are

you here and he isn't? I've gotten kind of used to seeing him shadowing your every move for the last couple of weeks or so," Lucy confessed.

Toni moved around the room, not knowing what to do with herself. "He's chasing a tip."

"What kind of tip?" Lucinda asked, obviously curious.

"The kind that's too dangerous for me to follow up on, apparently," Toni bit out. She sat down only to get up again. She couldn't seem to find a place for herself.

Having Lucinda grin at her like that certainly didn't help any, she thought darkly.

"He's trying to protect you," the other young woman told her.

Was that supposed to comfort her? Well, it didn't. Turning, she saw the expression on Lucinda's face. "What *are* you grinning about?"

Lucinda shook her head, clearly amazed that Toni was oblivious to this. "Don't you see? This proves that he really cares about you."

"No, it doesn't!" Toni argued. "What this proves is that he doesn't want me getting in the way."

Lucinda shifted around so that she was in front of Toni again, then cocked her head, staring at her. "You're not really that dumb, are you?"

Toni's head instantly jerked up as her eyes narrowed. Lucinda had never spoken to her like that before. "What?"

Lucinda didn't back off. "You heard me. I have

always looked up to you, Toni, thought you were the most talented, prettiest, most intelligent woman I had ever met. After all this time, are you going to make me reevaluate my initial impression of you?" she asked. "Because if you don't believe that man is crazy about you, then you're not as smart as I thought you were."

Toni blew out a breath. She knew exactly what Lucinda's judgment was based on.

"Sleeping with someone doesn't mean you're crazy about them," she said flatly.

"In general, no," Lucinda readily agreed. "But one look at that man's face when he's looking at you and I just *know* Detective Cavanaugh's crazy about you."

"Right," Toni bit off. "Whatever you say." Her tone completely dismissed the subject. "Anything else you want to talk about?"

Lucy thought for a moment, then came up with something neutral to mention. "Well, I think that Heather's cutting her first tooth."

"What? Why didn't you say so?" Toni cried, already on her way to the stairs.

"I just put her down for her nap," Lucy protested, coming up behind Heather's mother.

"I'm in crisis mode. I need a distraction," Toni said. But halfway up the stairs, she stopped and turned around. She was being selfish, she thought. "I guess I should add 'lousy mother' to the list," she said, frowning. "I was about to wake up the baby just to satisfy my own curiosity."

"But you stopped," Lucinda pointed out. "And there is no list, Toni. You're wonderful at everything you do, you know that. C'mon," she coaxed. "Why don't you come and help me make dinner?"

Toni glanced at her watch. "Isn't it kind of early to be making dinner?" she asked.

"Okay, an early dinner, then," Lucinda said, relenting. "Or we can call it a late lunch if it makes you feel better."

Toni laughed, shaking her head. "Sounds good." She appreciated Lucinda tolerating her behaving this way. She turned to look at the younger woman. "Why do you put up with me?"

Lucinda looked at her, her expression growing somber. "Because you saved my life," she answered simply. "And besides," she added, "you are the nicest person I ever met."

Toni's mood lifted a little and she put her arm around the younger woman's shoulders. "You really need to get out more."

"Something wrong, Cavanaugh?" Jason Nguyen asked. He and half of the team were encamped around what they had discovered was the exit point for one of the tunnels.

Beneath them was three quarters of a mile of freshly constructed walls and floor set deep in the bowels of the earth. What they'd initially found there would have made any contractor proud. The department had concluded that it took a specialized group of men to construct these passageways so that men and drugs could go safely from point A to point B.

Dugan thought of it as wasted talent.

Right now, though, Dugan's mind was on something else. He was working his lower lip, trying to decide whether or not he should be concerned or if he was worrying needlessly.

He looked at his partner. "I just called the officers who are supposed to be acting as Toni's bodyguards. I told them to be posted on either end of her block."

"And?" Nguyen asked, waiting for more.

Dugan frowned. "And they're not answering their cells."

Nguyen shrugged. "It's probably nothing. She probably invited them in for dinner. It would be the kind of thing that she'd do. She's really nice like that."

He knew she was, but he still felt uneasy. "They wouldn't both go in," he said, frowning. "They know better."

"Yeah, but she can be pretty persuasive," Detective Wayne Patterson said, overhearing the conversation and speaking up. He came over to join the other two detectives.

Dugan shook his head. "I don't know," Dugan confessed. "I've got a bad feeling about this."

"Oh, lord, not a gut feeling," Nguyen groaned, rolling his eyes. "Look, were the officers there when you left?"

"Yes. At least, their cars were," Dugan amended.

And then his eyes widened as it dawned on him. How could he have forgotten? "Their cars."

Patterson wasn't following him. "What about their cars?"

"I didn't check them," Dugan realized. Toni had gotten him angry and he'd just taken off. That wasn't like him. "I should have checked them before I left."

"Did anything look suspicious?" another member of the team, Detective Ramon Gomez asked, putting in his two cents.

"No," Dugan answered.

"Then give yourself a break and stop worrying," Nguyen advised. "This whole operation has you second-guessing yourself."

But once the thought had been planted in Dugan's head, it wasn't about to leave.

Dugan tried calling the police officers' cell phones again. "Still no answer," he complained, terminating the call after more than a dozen rings.

"You want to call dispatch and have them send someone to check it out?" Nguyen asked.

"Yeah," Dugan answered. He was already heading toward his vehicle. "Me."

"What if all this turns out to be nothing?" Nguyen called after him.

"Then I'll look pretty stupid, but I'll be relieved," Dugan said just before he closed his car's door.

Heather had woken up cranky. But after being changed and fed, then played with, the baby was placated. Before long, she began to drift off to sleep again.

"I think I fed her too much," Toni said. "All that formula made her drowsy," she speculated. "I should have taken the bottle away sooner."

"Babies are the best judge of when they're full," Lucinda said. "She's too young to need comfort food yet," she pointed out, trying to make Toni feel better about the situation.

Most of the dishes from dinner had been washed and were in the process of being put away. There was only one large pot left to deal with. Toni ran hot water into it, soaking the pot to make it easier to clean.

"How come you know so much about babies?" she asked Lucinda, feeling rather inadequate right now.

"I helped raise three younger siblings before I screwed up, remember?" Lucinda answered her matter-of-factly.

Toni winced, hearing the note of self-blame in the other woman's voice. After all this time, Lucinda still hadn't forgiven herself.

Drying her hands with a kitchen towel, Toni confided, "Well, I really don't know how I would have managed without you. I—"

She stopped abruptly, listening. Was that a noise coming from inside the house?

"Something wrong?" Lucinda asked, putting the last of the plates into the cupboard.

Whatever she'd heard was gone. Toni shrugged.

It was probably something from the house next door. "Nothing, I guess. I just thought I heard—"

She stopped again. Whatever she had heard, she was hearing it again. Her breath stopped in her chest. Dugan had definitely spooked her, but she couldn't shake the feeling that something was wrong.

"Lucy," she said, her voice lowering just a shade, "why don't you go upstairs to the nursery and lock the door while I check things out?"

"But we have a security system," Lucy pointed out, falling back on that comforting fact. "We're safe in here, right?"

"Right," Toni confirmed in a deliberately cheerful voice. "I'm just being overly cautious. So humor me," she requested, then added, "Please."

Lucinda looked at her for a minute before hurrying up the stairs.

Toni heard the younger woman enter the nursery, then heard the click that occurred when she locked the nursery door. Confident that Lucinda had followed her instructions, she went to the living room window and peered out.

Everything looked just the way it did before. There was nothing to suggest that there was anything really wrong.

She couldn't see either of the police cars, but in order to see them, she knew she needed to open the front door and go outside. Right now, that didn't feel like a good idea.

"Damn you, Dugan, you've got me spooked. Are you happy now?" she muttered under her breath.

Feeling uneasy, she called the police officer's cell. Dugan had given her the number just before she'd gotten out of his car. Each unanswered ring made her more nervous. She stopped at the tenth one.

This wasn't right, she told herself.

She moved back toward the front door and checked the keypad. The security system was armed.

The walk to the rear door and the other keypad felt as if it took forever. When she finally reached it, she found that the door was still locked.

All that uncertainty Dugan had planted in her head was getting the better of her. So what if the police officers he'd left posted outside her house weren't answering their cells? There could be a dozen reasons why they weren't picking up.

A dozen, she insisted to herself.

So why was her skin suddenly crawling?

And why did her stomach feel tied up in one big knot?

*You're making yourself crazy. There's no one in the house except for you and Lucy and the baby,* she told herself. *Heather's in her crib and there's nobody else here. It's just your imagination. Or it's the wind. The house creaks sometimes, remember? It's—*

She let loose with a scream. Turning around, she found herself looking at a thin five-foot-seven man. He was standing in her living room.

The same man who had entered the restaurant that night.

The most sinister-looking smile was curving the dark-haired man's lips. His dark-brown eyes were gleaming with a relish that instantly made her blood run cold.

"What are you doing here in my house?" she demanded, forcing herself not to sound intimidated.

"That is not a very hospitable way to greet a guest, Antonia," the invader chided. He was obviously enjoying the fact that he had caught her by surprise and that she was visibly nervous.

"How did you get in?" she asked. "I've got a security system."

The smile grew nastier. "Oh, please, you cannot be that naive, can you?" he mocked. "The system is pure child's play for someone like me."

She had to hide her fear, Toni told herself. He'd pounce on her if he saw fear. She threw back her shoulders, doing her best to sound angry.

"There are police officers outside," she told him. It worked, her terror was evolving into anger. "You should get out now while you still can," she ordered.

"There *were* police officers outside," Padilla corrected smugly. "I am afraid that they cannot hear you. Or help you," he added with a laugh that echoed with pure evil.

She thought she was going to throw up. Supreme effort kept down the bile that rose in her throat.

"I don't believe you," she said, doing her best to brazen it out.

"I do not particularly care if you believe me or not," Padilla said dismissively. His eyes darkened. "That is not why I am here."

Again her breath caught in her throat. *Breathe, damn it, breathe!* "Why are you here?"

"Oh, I think you know why," he told her. He appeared to be getting a great deal of pleasure from drawing the moment out. It was as if he was feeding on her fear and he was doing his best to terrify her. "Are you alone in the house?"

"Yes," Toni answered instantly, never taking her eyes off him.

"You said that a little too quickly," Padilla judged. "Tell me, if I went upstairs right now, who would I find there?"

"No one," she snapped. "But go ahead. Go look," she urged him. "I've got weapons stashed all around the house. It'll give me time to get one and use it on you," she declared.

"You are a regular little spitfire, I see. I should have guessed as much when you shot me in the restaurant." The smile on his lips was cold, frightening. "Too bad your aim was not so good."

She said the first thing that came to mind, trying to keep him talking until—she didn't know until what, she realized, but the longer he talked, the longer she stayed alive and that was at least something. "I wasn't trying to kill you."

"Really?" he asked, the single word mocking her. Laughing at her. "Then why would you bother shooting at all?"

"To stop you," she answered. That seemed pretty clear to her. "You just killed Oren and his bodyguard, and you looked like you were going to kill me next."

Padilla inclined his head. "Very smart, Antonia. I did not get a chance to kill you that night." And then the drug lord cocked the weapon he was holding. "But now is a different story. And once I kill you, I am going to kill that pretty little girl and that baby who are hiding upstairs."

## *Chapter Twenty-One*

Toni felt hot and cold at the same time and struggled not to allow either sensation to overwhelm her. Not to allow her growing fear engulf her. Above all else, she needed to find a way to distract this man, to keep her daughter and Lucinda safe.

She couldn't fail them.

Toni desperately wanted to run, but she stood her ground.

She had to.

"That's not fair," Toni cried angrily. "You leave them out of this, you hear me? They didn't do anything to you."

Padilla laughed, as if her protest was pathetic as well as ludicrous.

"I am not in the business of being fair," he told

her. "Fair does not matter. Only winning matters." He aimed his weapon at her.

What happened next was one huge blur.

Toni remembered hearing Padilla talk about killing her baby and Lucinda, and then suddenly it was as if she was watching some other woman reacting to the words, to the threat.

Lowering her head, she came charging at the drug lord, acting like a woman possessed with only one thought in her head: saving her baby and her friend.

"What the—" Padilla never had a chance to finish the angry sentence.

Catching him by surprise, Toni tackled Padilla. His gun discharged, with the bullet whizzing by her before it hit the wall. Toni scrambled for possession of the gun, but Padilla managed to catch her by her leg, pulling her away from the weapon before she could get her hands on it.

Twisting around, Toni kicked him as hard as she could with her free foot, her blow landing somewhere in his chest, temporarily knocking the air out of him.

"You bitch!" he rasped, wheezing as he cursed at her.

Struggling to catch his breath, he grabbed Toni in a vice-like hold. He began squeezing her as hard as he could.

Gasping for breath, instead of pulling away, she moved into his grip. Her face against his, she sank her teeth into his ear, biting down as hard as she could. She could taste blood.

Padilla screamed, letting her go. She instantly

scrambled back up and ran to the kitchen. All she could think of was getting hold of a knife in order to protect herself.

Meanwhile, Padilla had his gun back. "No, you don't!" he shouted at her, firing.

Again, he just narrowly missed her. If she hadn't moved, the shot would have caught her dead center. However, when she'd jerked aside, she wound up against the cabinets.

"Nowhere to run now," Padilla laughed. Her blood ran cold. "Looks like your luck has run out, bitch!"

"Not hers, yours," Dugan shouted, appearing behind him. His weapon was aimed right at Padilla. "Drop your weapon and turn around."

Padilla did whirl around, but he fired his gun as he did so.

Anticipating the move when he saw Padilla holding on to his weapon, Dugan shot back at him at the exact same moment.

His finger on his gun's trigger, Padilla reacted automatically, getting off one final shot just as he pitched forward. He was dead from a bullet to the head before he hit the floor.

Her heart pounding wildly, for one second Toni was immobilized, looking up at Dugan. The next second, she flung herself into his arms, holding on as tightly as she could.

"Are you okay?" he asked. "Are you hurt? Did he hurt you?"

Dugan was all but tripping over his tongue as the

realization that he could have actually lost her began to fully sink in.

When her heart stopped racing, Toni was finally able to draw back and look at Dugan. "How did you get here in time?" was all she was able to get out.

"By driving ninety miles an hour," he answered. And then he told her, "Lucy called me."

Her eyes widened before Dugan could say another word. "Oh, my God, Lucy!"

Breaking away from Dugan, Toni turned toward the stairs. It was at that point she realized that Dugan hadn't entered the house alone. There were two other officers with him.

Seeing the confusion in her eyes, he explained, "I called for backup on my way here."

Toni blinked, looking at the officers. Even in the midst of chaos, she was good with faces. "These aren't the officers who are supposed to be guarding the house, are they?" she asked, hating what her question implied.

"No," Dugan answered quietly, keeping his arm wrapped firmly around her. "Padilla killed them. Executed them where they sat in their squad cars," he told her. He was still beating himself up for not checking with the officers before he'd left, but he wasn't about to voice that now. His focus was on her, on making certain that she was all right. "You're safe, Toni," he told her. "Padilla won't be coming after you anymore."

She nodded her head, feeling numb and trying to deal with the aftermath of fear at the same time.

Toni pressed her lips together. "It's going to take me a while to stop shaking. I'm sorry."

He really wished he could have spared her this. "Nothing to be sorry about," he told her firmly, tightening his hold. "You just went through a really traumatic event—and you didn't fold up," he pointed out. "You fought back."

She looked at him, blinking back tears. She hardly heard him. Her mind was still on her daughter and friend upstairs. Her relief was huge.

"You saved Heather and Lucy," she told him.

"No," he contradicted. "You did. If you hadn't fought Padilla off, all three of you would have been dead by the time I got here, even though I was practically flying," he said.

Out of the corner of her eye, she saw Lucy coming down the stairs. Turning, she saw that Lucy had Heather in her arms and there was a young police officer with her. The latter seemed to be very taken with Lucy's safety as she made her way down the stairs.

The second Toni hit the landing, Lucinda was at her side, concerned. "Are you all right?" she cried, searching Toni's face.

"Yes, thanks to you and Dugan." Toni let out a long, shaky breath, turning toward Dugan. "So, it's really over?" she asked him. "His people aren't going to retaliate, are they?"

"Padilla wasn't the kind of leader who inspired that sort of loyalty," Dugan told her. Smiling, he added, "Although, just to be on the safe side, maybe I should stick around for a while."

And then his eyes narrowed as he looked at her more closely. Taking Toni's chin in his hand, Dugan turned her head so that he could get a better look at her left temple.

"You're bleeding." Moving back her hair from her face, he saw the thin line of blood that was only now appearing to grow thicker. "One of Padilla's bullets must have grazed you."

She shook her head. "I guess I didn't feel it in the heat of the moment." She looked over her shoulder, down the hallway. "I've got a first aid kit in the bathroom."

"First aid kit nothing," he told her heatedly. "I'm taking you to the hospital."

She put her hand on his shoulder, hoping to make him change his mind.

"Oh, please, I don't want to leave the house," she cried, looking toward Lucinda and her daughter. "Let's just stay here. I'll put a Band-Aid on this."

But Dugan was not about to be talked out of getting her to the hospital. He shot down any argument she was inclined to raise. "Lucy'll stay here with the baby," he told her. "And the officers will stay with them until we get back," he added.

Toni tried again. "But—"

"Don't argue with me, Toni. This isn't like the last time when I let you talk your way out of going to be checked out. You're going," Dugan insisted. "Even if I have to carry you there." Taking out his handkerchief, he wiped away the blood and then showed it to her, as if that should seal the discussion. "You're going."

"You wiped it all up," she told him, hoping that might get him to stand down.

He sighed, shaking his head. "You are probably the most infuriating woman I have ever met—and there are a lot of infuriating women in my family," he added. Dugan glanced at the officer standing next to a very concerned-looking Lucinda. "Miller, you and your partner stay here until I get back."

"Not a hardship, detective," Officer Miller replied with a wide smile.

"She's going to be all right, isn't she, Dugan?" Lucinda asked nervously.

"Don't worry. I'm not bringing her back until the doctor gives her a clean bill of health," Dugan promised the younger woman.

Just then, Heather began crying.

Toni looked up at Dugan. "My baby needs me."

"Yes, she does. But she needs you alive," he pointed out. There was no arguing with his tone when he said, "You're coming with me to the hospital."

"They'll just put a Band-Aid on it and charge me five hundred dollars," Toni told him, still attempting to get him to change his mind and let her take care of the wound herself. "I can do that and it won't cost five hundred dollars."

"Don't worry about it," he told her sternly. "I'll

pay for it. Now, if you're out of excuses—" he took her hand in his "—we're going to the hospital."

"Who says I'm out of excuses?" Toni protested as he drew her along in his wake.

He never even turned around to look at her. He simply said, "I do."

"Well, there's three hours of my life I'm never getting back," Toni complained when she was finally able to get back into his vehicle.

Dugan closed the passenger door and then rounded the hood to the driver's side. Getting in, he told her, "Better safe than sorry." He buckled up, glancing to make sure she had done the same. And then he paused to take a closer look at her bandage. "That's a lot bigger than a Band-Aid," he commented.

She frowned, shrugging. "I guess that they had to do something to make it look worth all that money they're charging."

His eyes swept over her. "You can drop the act now, Toni," he told her softly.

Toni seemed to pull into herself as she stuck her chin out, looking almost defiantly at him. "What act?"

Dugan didn't bother answering her retort. Instead, in a low voice he quietly admitted, "I was really scared, too."

Caught off guard, Toni wasn't sure how to answer him or what to think. "What?"

Because he wanted her to know exactly how he

had felt, Dugan went into detail. "When Lucy called me and said that Padilla had gotten into the house—"

"But she didn't know that," Toni protested. "I sent her upstairs to the nursery and told her to lock the door. She couldn't have seen him—he would have taken her prisoner if she'd crossed his path. And I never told her it was Padilla."

He smiled. "Lucy's a smart girl. She figured it out. She called me the second she got into the nursery and locked the door. Told me to come right away because you were in danger." He let out a shaky breath. "This was right after I had tried to reach the officers I left on your block. I don't even remember starting up the car."

Dugan took in a deep breath, as if to fortify himself against what he was about to relive. "When I got to your house and saw Padilla pointing his gun at you, I stopped breathing." His eyes met hers. "I was afraid I wasn't going to be able to get him before he got you."

"Well, luckily, you did," Toni said. She paused for a moment, trying to find the right words. "I didn't thank you for that, did I?"

He shrugged. "You don't have to."

"Oh, yes, I do," she insisted. "Thank you," she told him. Turning all the way toward him, she looked at Dugan for a long moment before saying, "Thank you for saving my life."

He laughed to himself. "Well, I kind of had to," Dugan admitted.

Toni nodded, thinking she understood what he

was telling her. She didn't want to draw this part out. "Because it's your job."

"No," he told her quietly, "because I couldn't have gone on living without you."

Her mouth nearly dropped open, but she collected herself just in time. Her throat was raspy as she said, "Excuse me?"

"You heard me," Dugan answered. "If anything had happened to you, if that worthless piece of garbage and human misery had managed to kill you, I couldn't have gone on."

No, she wasn't going to set herself up just to be disappointed, Toni told herself. He didn't mean it the way it sounded.

"Sure, you could have," she told him, refusing to allow herself to get carried away.

"Maybe I didn't make myself clear—" He stopped, then laughed. Not at her but at himself. "Hell, I *know* I didn't make myself clear. I just took it for granted that since you were so smart, you'd figure it out without my having to say a word."

"Figure what out?" she asked.

He took her hand, his eyes on hers. "That I love you."

"That you…"

Her voice trailed off as she stared at him. It was one thing to kind of hope that her suspicions had a chance of being right. It was another thing entirely to hear the words.

"That I love you," Dugan repeated. He searched her face, waiting for a reaction. She looked as if she was completely numbed over. "Is that so terrible?" he asked her.

It took her a minute to find her voice.

"Well, yes," she finally said, "if this is some kind of elaborate joke on your part."

He supposed that he didn't blame her for being skeptical. In her place, he would probably feel the same. He'd never given her a reason to feel otherwise.

"I kid about a lot of things," Dugan admitted. "But joking about falling in love with someone has never been one of them. Love's too special," he told her. "To be honest, I really never thought it would happen to me. I watched my cousins find that certain someone to complete them, but I figured that the odds were pretty much against me doing the same."

"Why?"

"Because finding someone to love, someone who makes you glad to *be* alive, that's something that happens in the movies and once in a rare while in real life. But that doesn't mean it has to happen to me. And it didn't—until now," he told her. He saw the expression on her face. She looked like she was beaming. "What?"

"You know, for a police detective, you have got one silver tongue."

Dugan laughed. "No one's ever accused me of that before."

"Then I guess I'm the first," she told him.

"The first for a lot of things," he readily admitted. "The first woman whose baby I delivered. The first woman I ever fell in love with."

She felt a smile warming her as she nodded her head. "I think I can handle that," she told him. "Especially the last part."

His mouth curved. "You're sure?"

"Oh, very sure," she told him. And then she looked around outside of his vehicle. They were still parked in the rather small ER parking lot. "Don't you think that maybe we should start the car so you can get out of this spot?"

"In a minute," he told her. "But I've got something else to do first."

She wasn't sure she understood. "Like what?" she asked.

"Like this," he told her. And then he took her into his arms and kissed her.

Neither one of them came up for air for a long while.

# Epilogue

With the threat to her life over, Toni was allowed to come back to work with the team. However, her job description had changed. She was there now to document the takedown of a branch of the newly flourishing American segment of the Juarez Cartel.

After several more weeks of following up on tips, a number of lower-end workers and one higher-end drug lord were finally caught utilizing one of the cartel's supertunnels, originally made famous by the Sinaloa Cartel. The supertunnels were used to transport huge shipments of drugs to destinations so that they could be flown to other parts of the Southwest.

"This haul has got to be worth at least several million dollars," Toni marveled that evening after the takedown had happened.

"It's admittedly a drop in the bucket," Dugan allowed. "But at least it is a drop and every shipment that *doesn't* hit the streets is a victory for our side."

She nodded, clearing away the dishes. Bringing over a bottle of wine, she sat down again. Dugan did the honors and poured them each a glass.

"So now what?" she asked.

"We celebrate," he said, nodding at the two glasses. "And then we hit the streets tomorrow to hopefully do it all over again."

"Sounds exhausting," she freely admitted, taking a sip from her glass.

He smiled at her. "It has its rewards."

She had a feeling he wasn't talking about drug busting any more. "You know, Lucinda's pretty taken with that police officer."

Dugan already knew that. "Well, between you and me, he's pretty taken with her." Lucinda had left with the officer earlier to have dinner out. "What is this, their second date?" he asked.

"Third," Toni corrected. She toyed with the wine in her glass, smiling. "I've got a good feeling about this," she confided. "Lucy needs someone like Patrick in her life."

"Patrick?" he questioned.

"Officer Miller," she told him. "They actually come with first names, you know."

Dugan inclined his head. "Right." And then he looked at her. "So, you have a feeling about them?" he questioned. "A *gut* feeling?"

"Yes, I do. I know, you're going to make fun of it, aren't you?" she said, second-guessing his reaction.

"Not at all. I was just going to ask you if you have any more of those gut feelings."

"About what?" she asked cautiously, not sure what he was after.

He took a breath. "I'm asking if you have any gut feelings about us."

"About us?" she echoed, rather surprised that he'd ask something like that. "I'm not sure what you want me to say."

"Anything you want to say," he answered, trying his best to sound nonchalant about it. "I'm just exploring the subject. *Do* you have a gut feeling about us?" he asked.

"I know that I'm grateful to you for saving my life *and* for delivering my baby," she said, steering away from the actual question. "I'm never going to be able to pay you back for that."

"I'm not asking to be paid back," he told her, clearly frustrated at the direction this conversation was going.

"Then what *are* you asking for?" she asked.

Her voice was low and it felt as if it was undulating under his skin, arousing him.

"You," he answered softly, the single word throbbing with emotion.

"Go on," she coaxed.

He ran his hand through his hair, restless. For the first time in his life, he felt as if he was at a complete loss. His words were deserting him.

"You're making this hard," he complained.

"No, I'm not," she countered. "What about me?" she asked.

When she looked at him like that, there was only one answer he could give. "I want you."

Toni could feel her heart accelerating, but she forced herself to sound calm.

"For how long?"

"How does forever sound?" he asked.

She was afraid of jumping to the wrong conclusion. *Baby steps, Toni. Baby steps.* "You want to move in?" she asked.

"Yes, of course I do," he answered. "Husbands and wives usually live together."

For a second, the world froze. She blinked, shaking her head. "Hold it, back up. I think you missed a step there," she said, shaken.

Dugan flushed. "I forgot to ask you to marry me, didn't I?"

She could feel herself melting. He was adorable. "Um, yes, you did."

Suddenly it was his turn to be nervous. Nervous because he had all but already asked her and she hadn't said anything one way or the other, other than to point out that he *hadn't* actually asked. Which meant she could still say no and he'd be left standing here, not knowing what to say next or how to make an exit without looking like a complete idiot.

"So? Are you going to ask?" Toni prompted.

Maybe she wouldn't say no, after all. Dugan took a deep breath as if he was about to dive into the deep end of the pool, and said, "Toni O'Keefe, will you marry me?"

She wanted to scream "Yes!" but there was one point that had to be made clear—just in case. "You realize that I come as a set, don't you?"

He looked at her, puzzled. Did she think he forgot that?

"Of course I realize that. I love that baby of yours just as much as I love you," he told her. "So?" he asked uneasily when she didn't say anything. "Is it yes?"

That was when he saw it, the smile that formed in her eyes before it ever reached her lips.

"You dummy, it's been yes from the night that you delivered Heather," she told him, throwing her arms around his neck.

Relieved, he told her, "You could have led off with that."

"And miss seeing you sweat out this proposal? Not on your life, Cavanaugh," she laughed.

Toni stopped laughing. The sound disappeared the second that he kissed her.

She didn't laugh for a long time.

\* \* \* \* \*

# COMING SOON!

We really hope you enjoyed reading this book. If you're looking for more romance, be sure to head to the shops when new books are available on

## Thursday
## 12th July

To see which titles are coming soon, please visit
**millsandboon.co.uk**

# LET'S TALK
## *Romance*

For exclusive extracts, competitions
and special offers, find us online:

**f** facebook.com/millsandboon

**◉** @millsandboonuk

**𝕏** @millsandboon

Or get in touch on 0844 844 1351*

For all the latest titles coming soon, visit
millsandboon.co.uk/nextmonth

# Want even more
# ROMANCE?

## Join our bookclub today!

'Mills & Boon books, the perfect way to escape for an hour or so.'

Miss W. Dyer

'Excellent service, promptly delivered and very good subscription choices.'

Miss A. Pearson

'You get fantastic special offers and the chance to get books before they hit the shops'

Mrs V. Hall